Gifted

Silversmith
PUBLISHING

For information on new and upcoming books,
go to **mmarinanbooks.com**

Gifted

A Fairytale Memoirs novella

M. MARINAN

First published in New Zealand in 2019
by Silversmith Publishing

A catalogue record for this book is available from the National Library of New Zealand

ISBN 978-0-9951108-8-5

*Inspired by French fairytale 'La Belle et la Bete'
(Beauty and the Beast).*

For Mum.
*There's a reason fairytale characters are so often orphaned
– because if parents are there to do their jobs, there'll be
far less danger and drama. Thank you for doing your job
well, and for letting me read so many books as a kid.*

*And as always, thanks to Anne-Marie and Kate
for helping to shape and polish this story.*

Key:
COUNTRY
(Novel)

NORDANTE
(Gifted)

Veestlun

ENORIA
(Gifted)

THE
WINTER
SEA

Hunting Lodge
The Aileron

DANVIA
(Rose Red)

BRESA

GENTRAVIA

DELMANY
*(Viola Sends
Her Regrets)*

Leewhey

OSTRAIME

THE
SUMMER
SEA

Fortrente

Novas · Strenley

The
Fairytale
Memoirs
Map

CRISTONIA
(Viola Sends Her Regrets:
The Hundred-Layer Quilt)

BRELFNE
(Bluebeard's
Last Wife)

CRISTON

LANCASTRE

SUDANTE
The Red Desert

Contents

1
The Letter

Enorian tent settlement, South Nordante,
1673 FTE (fairytale era)

The letter crumpled in my tightly clenched fist, and as I looked up at my companions, I realised I was shaking. Master and Missus Streeth were the leaders of our nomadic group. They wore the same dusty brown colour as I did; the same dusty brown as the tents we stood in. Master's lined face was creased with worry, and Missus's with anger. I'd known her long enough to see that her anger *was* worry – for me.

But the other person standing in the tent... He was young, and as pale in colour as were all the Nordante locals. Compared to our golden skin and black hair, his looked like he'd been left out in the rain until the dye ran out. His clothing was more cheerful though: green and yellow. He met my eyes with his own weird, light grey ones, and I struggled to hold that gaze for a moment before looking away.

"Well?" Master Streeth demanded. "What does it say, Claire? This *boy* wouldn't let us look at it, said it had to go to one of Alden's daughters."

Alden being my father, and me being the oldest and most responsible of his three girls. "Um," I began. I swallowed.

Would the Veest emissary be offended at being called a 'boy' like that? He was tall and skinny, sort of half-grown in appearance, but he looked so serious. "It's from Father. He says that he's well."

"Come on, Claire," Missus Streeth prompted. "He wouldn't have written just to say he was well, even though those *Veest* are keeping him hostage and of course we'd want to know. What do they want?"

"Peace," the boy said, speaking for the first time since I'd answered the Streeths' summons. I could feel his eyes on me. Was he judging me in contrast to the requirements outlined on the letter? "Peace between our people. A place for yours to settle, and so that ours may hunt and travel freely in our ancestral lands without fear of getting an arrow in the head." There was a moment where I could see the confusion in Master and Missus's expressions, and the emissary wasn't helping at all. That was such a vague answer.

"An arrow in the head?" Master Streeth said in a low voice. "That was only once. How many of ours have you killed or injured? We just want to *live* here, not fight! The war comes from your side!"

Oh, help. This was *not* the way to make lasting peace. I didn't know about Father's suggestion, either, but... "Marriage," I blurted out. "They want to join our peoples by marriage. The son of their ruler, to the daughter of ours."

The Streeths' eyebrows shot up in identical startled expressions. "But we don't have any girls," Missus pointed out. "And we don't have an official ruler. We just lead the meetings because...well, no one else does it."

And that was pretty much how our people worked. About fifty of us had grown tired of the constant corruption, famine and drought in our tiny country of Enoria, and headed north. Two years later we'd made our way far into the mountains of the neighbouring kingdom, and were yet to find a decent place to settle that wasn't already taken. This area in the south-east of Nordante was damp, green and wild in more ways than one. And the locals, who called themselves the Veest? Wilder still.

"Then the daughter of one of your high-ranking officials," the Veest emissary said. Out the corner of my eye I could see he was studying me speculatively. "This one is too young, I think. Is there an older sister?"

I didn't flinch, well accustomed to that kind of comment. As for the Streeths, they didn't point out that we didn't *have* any high-ranking officials. Father was respected by our people, and perhaps that was the next best thing.

"Too young for who or what, exactly?" Missus demanded stridently. "Claire here is seventeen, coming up eighteen, for all that she looks twelve. Her mother was the same. Besides, we're not all as enormous as you lot."

Did I look twelve? I'd argue for fourteen. Some people just grew short and round-cheeked. Especially me. "Peace," I said again quickly. "That's the goal, right? Father has found a lovely valley, a lush, uninhabited one on the edge of the Veest lands. And if we can all get on, then we can settle. Build houses, plant crops for the first time in years."

"We know what our goals are," Master cut in gruffly. "We've been planning this since you really were twelve, missy." He turned to the emissary. "Look, whatever your name is-"

"Damon." The Veest pronounced it like 'Day-mon'.

"Damon. How long have we got before you folks start slicing and dicing our Alden?"

A twinge of fear twisted my belly. That was my *father* they were talking about. My only surviving parent! He'd headed out a few weeks earlier to try to find us a better place to settle, and had been captured by the locals instead. I was glad they hadn't hurt him – but I didn't know how long that would last. I turned to stare at the emissary. "Well?"

"And bear in mind that we've got you here too," Missus added quickly. "Your people hurt Alden, and you won't be going home either."

Oh, they looked so very fierce while they said it, even though they were both half a head shorter than him. But if

3

he was a shapeshifter and could become a bear, a wolf, or an eagle, then what could we do?

But Damon's pale eyebrows shot up. "Peace," he said again, enunciating the word in his strange accent. We all spoke the same language, but even if we hadn't looked so different, we would have known it by those tones. "That means no, er, slicing and dicing."

"How long, boy?"

He shrugged. "I'm expected back within two days. We'd need a decision by sunset."

It was midday now, and the sun was high in the sky, warming our already-warm plain to baking level. It wasn't as bad as what I remembered from Enoria, because there was plenty of water here, but it wasn't comfortable either.

But I thought of my father again, and of my two younger sisters. If Father was killed, then they'd be orphans. *I'd* be an orphan, and our people would have to leave...again. "I'd do it without hesitation to save my father's life," I said. "But I don't think I fit the requirements." I handed the letter over to Missus, and she and her husband leaned in to read it. I could see her squinting to make out the text, and his lips moving slightly. The problem wasn't Father's handwriting, which was quite tidy. It was the content.

After a minute Missus looked up at me frankly. "I see what you mean. Ah, well. It's not like we've got single beauties to throw around, have we?"

I shrugged, but inside my heart was beating double-time. This wasn't about me. It was about Father, and about everyone. We needed a home. We needed *peace.*

She sighed, then handed me back the letter. "Go see your sisters, Claire. We'll talk a little more with this lad here."

At least he'd graduated from just being 'the Veest'.

I nodded, then left. I already knew what I was going to do, but it didn't mean everyone else was going to like it.

"I don't see why we can't just stay here," my sister Tabitha said staunchly. She folded her slender arms in front of her chest, pouting. At fifteen she was a mere eighteen months younger than me, but her temperament wasn't nearly as relaxed. Hopefully she'd grow out of it. "There's water here, and you wouldn't have to marry anyone."

I sighed, moving over to my side of the small tent to sort through my meagre belongings. "Water, yes, but the land is made of rocks. We can't grow anything here, and the summers would be brutal. The place Father found – the others say it's beautiful. Green, a little damp. Things would grow like crazy. We could build homes…"

"Ned says you shouldn't marry an animal," Tabitha cut in. "That would be disgusting. Your children would be hairy. Maybe some of them would have *tails*!"

Ned being her 'betrothed'. He was fifteen too, and just as outspoken. Unlike her, he didn't seem to have the kindness that made her bearable, and the rest of the family had been unhappy when they'd announced themselves betrothed last winter. They couldn't marry until they were sixteen, of course, but I was hoping that either they changed their minds, or Ned fell off a cliff before then. (Ha, ha.) Except here was the upside of that betrothal – Tabitha, who was rather closer to the 'beauty' requirement, was already taken. I considered that a good thing. I'd bet that if my sister was in the Veest city for more than a day, she'd have started a war for real. And with us being outnumbered ten to one? We'd lose.

"They don't have tails, Tab," I said patiently. "They look human. They just turn into animals sometimes."

"Disgusting!" she announced again.

I rolled my eyes, turning back to my clothing. Now what should I pack? Brown dress one, brown dress two, slightly lighter brown dress three…and my dowry, which was my late mother's silver comb and matching mirror. I'd always figured that one day I'd take the 'wealth' to my new husband. And unless the emissary turned me down, that day would be tomorrow.

"I think it's alright," my youngest sister Amadine said from where she sat near my feet. She was only ten, and looked more like me than Tabitha: small and round-faced, with wide dark eyes. "Maybe they'd be like puppies. I like puppies."

Tabitha opened her mouth to no doubt say something scathing, and I cut in. "Don't you want to hear the letter?"

"Yes," Amadine piped in. "Did Father send us a present with it? I asked for a jewel." Meaning a pretty rock to add to her collection.

"And I asked for a new dress, not that I'm likely to get that," Tabitha retorted. "What does it say, Claire?"

I unrolled the parchment once more, carefully setting aside the squashed yellow rose that was wrapped inside. Ironically, that had been what I'd asked for. A rose. This was worse-for-wear, but still fragrant.

"Dear girls," I began to read. "I trust you are all well. I have good news. Rose Valley looks even better on closer inspection, and it will surely be a perfect location for our new village. Even better, the local Veest that I've met are very keen on making peace after the bloodshed of the last few months." I paused, taking a breath. By now I'd read this over and over, and it was the next part that still made me twitch.

"Yes, we know that," Tabitha prompted when the silence dragged on for too long. "What's the next part?"

I continued, "As you're by now aware, I've been taken into the care of the Veest. They say they're tired of the skirmishes, and want to broker true peace between us. The ruler of the city, Kanut, thinks that if one of our girls marries his son, then we'll not want to fight anymore, and I daresay he's right. They've requested a high-born, sweet-natured, beautiful maiden as bride."

There was a long pause as my sisters and I all looked at each other. Then Tabitha's nose wrinkled. "Stars above, that's a big ask. There are what, five girls of marriageable age? Three of those are already betrothed, including me. And then there's you and Halley."

Halley was sweet-natured, that was for sure. She was also simple – with the mind of a child – and no more 'high-born' than any of the rest of us. "So there's really no choice," I said again. I didn't bother to read the rest of the letter aloud, for we already knew what it contained. "I might not be a beauty, but who else will do it?"

"I think you're beautiful," Amadine said staunchly. She set her arms around my waist. "But I don't want you to go!"

"The Veest city isn't that far from Rose Valley," I replied calmly. I put my arms around her comfortingly, but inside I was as tense as a drawn spring. "I'll see you all the time. It'll be an adventure."

"But would Father really want you to go?" Tabitha asked. "I mean, he wouldn't want you to sacrifice yourself to a *Veest*. He wouldn't make you do something that horrible."

"That's not true," Amadine interrupted. "He makes me go to bed early every time there's a feast, and he even made me eat a whole plate of horrible sprouts once, just because Missus Bloomer made them and he wanted to please her. Remember?"

"Nobody cares about your sprouts, Amadine," Tabitha cut in tersely, pushing her hand over the younger girl's mouth to silence her. "And Claire, he wouldn't want you to do something that *dangerous*. The Veest aren't even real people! For all we know, they're cannibals! We could end up roasted on a spit!"

I didn't point out that in order to be cannibals they'd need to eat their own kind, therefore saving us. Instead I sighed, my tone not betraying my twisting gut. I could see where this was going, and I didn't like it. "Don't be ridiculous, Tab. There's no evidence that the Veest have ever eaten a human."

"Only because no eaten human ever got a chance to tell anyone about it!"

There was a long, heavy silence interrupted by a scuffle as my youngest sister tried to shove my middle sister's hand away from her face, and succeeded. She was a lot smaller, but she was determined, and there may have been some saliva involved.

"If they don't eat people, I wouldn't mind marrying one," Amadine announced. "I could have chocolate cake and wear a white dress."

Oh, what a lovely, innocent view of marriage. If only it was about chocolate cake rather than avoiding war. And as for white dresses – nobody wore white back home in Enoria; it was asking for trouble. We all wore boring, boring brown so the marks didn't show when our skirts dragged through the dust. But here in this foreign kingdom, we'd actually started thinking about a better life...until the locals decided they didn't want us living so close. These last few years had been precarious, and finally having peace would be a miracle. All we had to do was send a bride...

"They don't want to eat us," I pointed out as mildly as I could in the circumstances. "I believe the letter states that they want to marry one of us. And as I'm the only one who isn't already taken – or far too young – I suppose that means me."

"Stars above!" Tabitha exclaimed, tossing her long black hair over one shoulder. "You sound as if you don't even care that you might be marrying some sort of big, hairy beast within a month. Do you even have emotions, Claire?"

"I didn't say I don't care," I replied. "Besides, speaking of marrying big hairy beasts, you're betrothed to one and you don't seem to mind. It can't be that bad."

"Ned does need a haircut," Amadine agreed. "His hair covers his eyes sometimes."

"I can't believe you're comparing my betrothed to one of those- those *monsters!*" Tabitha spat, then as usual at this point in the argument, her face crumpled. "Oh stars, they're going to kill and eat Father unless you go and marry one of them. But how can you?"

How could I not? "I'm pretty sure they don't eat people," I said once again, hearing the terseness in my tone. "I was reading the reports that were written when we first arrived, and it said that a few of them are shapeshifters, but not cannibals."

"Always with the reading! Do you trust everything you read?"

"When it's a well-written, logical report by someone with actual experience, yes," I retorted. "Now if you don't mind, I'm going back to talk to the Streeths."

I made my way back to our meeting tent to find there was now quite a crowd. The Veest emissary stood quietly off to one side, watching us with a seeming lack of interest, but our people had already got into hot debate.

"Oh, let the girl do it!" someone said. "This is what we all need, isn't it? This is what we've been working towards."

"But will she be *safe*?" someone else cut in. "We don't know what those creatures are capable of!"

I coughed quietly. No one heard me, so I nudged the closest person, one of the younger, married girls. "Are they talking about me?"

"Claire!" She turned to the others, raising her voice. "Claire's here!"

Suddenly I was the centre of attention.

"Look at her," I heard one of the older ladies say. "She's so cute. Who would hurt her?"

I glanced across to where Damon stood. His expression hadn't changed. "My father wouldn't have written that letter if he thought it was dangerous," I said loudly. "He knew I was one of the only options, and he wouldn't have me put into a situation like that."

"Are you sure he wrote the letter?" the boy nearest me queried. His name was Alec, and he was seventeen like me, with typical Enorian black hair and eyes, and golden skin. He was also very handsome, and one of the few who weren't already wed or betrothed. Unfortunately his tastes didn't run to 'cute' – so my feelings weren't reciprocated. I felt my cheeks heat.

"Yeah, it's his," Missus Streeth said, saving me from answering. "He always smudges the ink."

"But what if he was forced to write it?" Alec challenged. He stared at the emissary. "Was he?"

Damon lifted his chin, apparently unconcerned. "He was

9

told that he could not leave until this bargain is completely fulfilled," he replied calmly. "And I have been instructed to give the same information. I will leave first thing tomorrow. If you wish to send one of your girls with me – a sweet-natured beauty, of course – then Master Alden will be free to go, and your people free to move into the valley unchallenged. If you do not wish to send one, then I will leave alone, and your Master Alden will stay with our people until our ruler decides otherwise."

I felt my cheeks redden a little more at the request for a 'sweet-natured beauty' being announced so loudly. "Can I talk to him in private, please?"

No one was keen on that idea, but Damon and I managed to move about ten feet away from the rest of the crowd. "Look," I said quietly. "We all know that we need your goodwill more than you need ours. And I'm quite fond of my father, and would also like him back. But really, honestly, would I do? Because we don't have anyone else." Damon looked up, and I saw his eyes settle on Tabitha where she stood at the edge of the crowd, watching us. "Anyone else *available*," I cut in. "You said you needed a maiden."

Oh, Tab would hate me for saying such a thing since I was pretty sure she and Hairy Ned had never gone there, but I was saving her. Hopefully she'd never find out.

The Veest turned back to me, looking me up and down. Then he shrugged. "Why not."

And that was that. I turned to move back to the others, but he set his hand on my arm. "Wait. Who was that boy you were talking to? The handsome one."

Now I really felt my cheeks heat. Generally I was hard to embarrass, but any mention of Alec would make me blush. "Alec is just another settler."

"No…*friendship*?"

"We're not really friends," I muttered, sparing a glance at Alec from the corner of my eye. He seemed to be arguing with Tabitha, something he did with enthusiasm. "But we know each other, as does everyone. There's nothing else to it."

"Hmm," Damon said. And that was all.

"You're a bold one," Missus Streeth declared that evening in the privacy of the main tent. "You might look small and sweet, but you've got a spine of steel. Providing they're not the beasts that people claim them to be, then you'll do well." She exchanged a glance with her husband, and her lips tightened unhappily. "But I don't like this. Your mother was my friend, and I don't think she would have liked it either, us sending you off to the Veest caves to have half-animal babies."

Then seeing my appalled expression, she sighed. She wasn't at her best in this chaos, but I knew she was a kind woman. "Oh, it might not be as bad as all that, Claire, but it's a big ask. Marrying a Veest? I hear they spend half their time as animals! Some of them might not even be able to change back, and they want us to send you into that?"

"It might not be true," I murmured half-heartedly, but even I didn't believe that. So I lifted my chin and said, "If I go, it will be by choice. I know you'd never make me. It's just..."

"You're afraid of a horrible death?"

"No!" No matter what anyone said, I was sure they weren't cannibals, and perhaps not even violent. Mostly sure. Just look at that boy with his too-pale colouring and calm manner. He looked too mild to ever devour anyone... "I was thinking about what Damon had said, about what sort of girl they were expecting. They might be disappointed if they end up with me.""Fishing for compliments, are we?"

My cheeks heated. "Of course not. I just meant that they seem to be expecting a beauty, and I'm..."

"Short, cute rather than pretty, and with no dress sense?"

Ouch. "I was going to say ordinary, but that's one way of putting it. And I can't see that my dress sense is any worse than anyone else's here." All our dresses turned the same shade of sun-bleached brown within a few months, and the sun had turned my skin to almost the same colour, and had put hints of brown in my curly black hair. Not a match with my name that meant 'pale', but that couldn't be avoided.

"That boy didn't seem to mind," Master Streeth pointed out. "Besides, how do you know what they'd find beautiful? Probably a girl with a face like a pig and hair like a wild dog. You'll be gorgeous in contrast."

I didn't point out that the Veest boy was hardly ugly, just pale. Instead I said, "It seems like we've got more to gain than lose here. I think I should go."

This time Missus Streeth didn't contradict me. Instead she looked across at her husband. "Well?"

"Let her go. Who knows, maybe we *will* be able to settle here. Sounds a good sight better than going back to that dust bowl we came from in Enoria."

Missus sighed. "Fine. But if they cause you trouble, Claire, you don't hold back, alright?" She made a fist to demonstrate, her thumb tucked outside her fingers, then jabbed at the air. "Just like we showed you. Nose, throat, gut or lower. Understood?"

"Understood," I replied a little dryly. They'd taught all of us girls – and boys – to defend ourselves, but up 'til now I'd never needed to use those skills. I hoped I could still say that in three months' time.

The news spread like wildfire – *Claire's going to marry a Veest!* – and I had more conversations that evening with some settlers than I'd had in a year. Everybody had to hear it for themselves, and repeating it over and over should have made it feel more real to me. But it didn't. It just felt like one of those articles I liked to read, the sort which would make me think 'isn't that interesting', and then would be forgotten about.

Of course my sisters cared that I was leaving, but they were more concerned about Father coming home, and that maybe we could all stay in this area after all and not have to pack up our lives once more in search of somewhere liveable. We'd – they'd – have to move a few hours north into

Rose Valley, but it was nothing compared to the travel we'd already done from Enoria.

I didn't have much I could take with me. We weren't rich, and all I had was just that silver comb and mirror from my mother. Pretty, but you couldn't exactly live off them. But then neither the letter nor the emissary had said anything about needing a dowry – just a bride.

A sweet-natured, beautiful, unmarried girl. Argh...at least I could claim the last requirement, pretend the second didn't matter, and fake the first.

I made my way back to my 'room', which was actually half of the tent I shared with my sisters. My space was cut off by a sheet hanging from the ceiling, and I was finally alone. Just me, my bedroll, and my few bundles of clothing. I unfolded the largest bundle to expose the aforementioned silver dowry, then picked up the mirror and idly studied my reflection.

Round brown cheeks, round dark eyes, curly black hair sticking to my forehead from the heat. Yep, all normal...except for those downturned lips. That wasn't normal, because I was starting to feel quite sorry for myself. Did anyone even care that I was leaving? Or was I just a convenient sacrifice?

Realising how that sounded, I twisted my lips in a half-amused, half-annoyed pout. "Don't be a martyr," I told my reflection. "You're choosing this, and you know what's at stake."

Peace with the Veest, *everyone* being able to settle somewhere safe and beautiful...and my father's freedom, unless they'd been joking about that. I didn't think they had been. So with that in mind, I could handle marrying a stranger who might also turn into a hairy beast on occasion. Maybe I could arrange to have him stay outside during those times, just like you wouldn't come inside with dirty boots.

I was still musing on exactly what waited for me when a light cough sounded from just outside. "Claire? Are you alone? It's Alec."

I'd recognised his voice immediately, and felt my

heartrate pick up. "Um, yes. Just…talking to myself." Damn. I hadn't meant to say that out loud.

There was a pause. "Can I come in?"

Of course he could! He was one of the few boys my age, and he was also one of the few I'd really miss. "Just a moment." I quickly checked my hair again in the mirror, decided that it wasn't going to get any better, then smoothed my hands over my plain brown skirts. "Come in."

There he was in all his tall, dark, handsome glory, right down to the thick-lashed dark eyes. He pushed aside the sheet/door, taking care to leave it hooked so that it was 'open'. It wouldn't do to have any rumours about the two of us alone in a bedroom right before I went off to get married – that would likely wreck the entire point of going, and for nothing. Alec wasn't interested in me that way. He'd made it more than clear in the past.

"Everyone's saying that you're leaving with that pasty-faced Veest," he said.

"Then everybody would be right," I replied, turning away to fold one of my better dresses, the one I used for celebrations. Perhaps it would be my wedding dress, white or not. "I go first thing in the morning."

"Just like that."

"Just like that," I repeated calmly.

"Were you even going to say goodbye?"

I looked up at him in surprise. Yes, he really did look annoyed, and that made me a little annoyed right back. "I wouldn't have thought it would make any difference to you. You never cared before."

"I cared, I just always thought…that you'd be here. I didn't think you'd just run off to marry some monster! Stars above, Claire! Do you think your life is worth this…this *peace* they say we'll get?"

"I am ninety-nine percent sure that I won't be killed, eaten or even maimed," I said lightly. "So yes, I think it is worth it. And we don't even know if my betrothed will be a shapeshifter. Maybe I can think of it as an adventure."

Alec stared at me intently. "I wish you wouldn't go."

Now a spike of irritation shot through me. His timing was terrible! "Oh, shall I tell them I have a previous commitment? Shall I stay and marry you, Alec, and we can find some other way to rescue my father and somewhere else to live that the Veest haven't already claimed? Or maybe we should just go back to Enoria, and make the hard work of the last few years for nothing."

I'd been sarcastic, but there was a part of me that was honest, too. I'd given him this chance to speak up about how he felt about me, but his silence gave the answer I'd expected. I turned away, regaining control of my temper and pretending to straighten the embroidered sheets I was adding to my bag. "Never mind. When it all works out and you lot can all finally build permanent homes in Rose Valley, then you'll see I did the right thing."

"And do you really think you'll be happy, married to one of those animals?"

"Well, he won't be an animal *all* the time," I retorted. "Now if you don't mind, I have some packing to do."

2
The Veest

I was up at first light the next morning, kissing my sisters goodbye and fixing a pleasant smile on my face. The Streeths and a couple of others got up to watch me go. Alec wasn't one of them.

As for Damon the Veest, he didn't have much to say once we got moving except, "Can you lean either forward or back? I can't see past your head."

I sat sideways in front of him on the horse, my small bags hanging from behind me, and I blushed a little, trying to get out of the way. "I'm surprised to see you have a horse. I would have thought-"

"That I'd turn into a wolf and run the whole way? Sorry to disappoint, but I don't have the gift."

"The gift...?"

"The ability to change into a wolf, a bear, an eagle, or one of the many other shapes that can be taken. Not all Veest do, you know. That's why it's called a gift, it's special."

"Special as in one in five have it?"

There was a long silence as if he was deciding whether to reply, then he said, "More like one in three. But I'm one of the ungifted."

"Why did they send you to us, then? You couldn't have defended yourself if my people had attacked."

I couldn't see his face, but I felt him flinch. "Maybe the same reason that you're coming with me," he answered lightly.

"And what's that?"

"You're agreeable...and you're expendable."

Now that was a conversation killer. I sat quietly, rocking with the movement of the horse and thinking...*expendable.*

I wasn't, was I? But I couldn't stop thinking about that, and about people turning into wolves or eagles or whatever Damon had said earlier. He didn't speak again either, so we just rode in silence until we stopped for lunch. We'd followed the road steadily upwards and around corners until the hills bordered us steeply on each side, but they'd changed quickly from brown tussock to purely green. I knew from my reading that landscapes could affect weather, but it was a shock to see it outworked so dramatically. The trees around us grew taller and lusher, and the smell of something lovely filled the air.

"Mm, what's that scent?" I asked.

"Peaches," Damon replied. "Help yourself, but be careful. There are wasps."

There were, but they didn't stop me from eating at least three. Peaches, that was, not wasps. I'd had very little fresh fruit in months, and these were small and thin-skinned with juicy yellow flesh – well worth risking any sting.

I was considering a fourth when a rumble from behind me made the hair stand up on the back of my neck. I lowered my hand and turned slowly. Right behind me was an enormous brown bear, easily seven feet tall, and watching me blankly with small black eyes.

I didn't react well. I froze with fear, and a squeak came out of my mouth. The peach I'd grabbed fell and rolled to land at the bear's feet.

It looked down, then back at me, then seemed to shrug before ambling off into the greenery. That was when I saw that Damon had been standing there the whole time, eyebrows raised. "You'll have to control yourself better than that when we arrive at my home. What will you do if you see

17

a Veest in animal form?"

"I didn't know it was a Veest," I finally managed to say. "I thought it was just a bear."

He didn't look impressed. "Around here, assume *everything* is a Veest, because if you don't you might be sorry. No hunting, no running or screaming, alright? Your betrothed's people carry this gift, so if you want peace then you'll need to learn better."

I swallowed. "I'm not betrothed yet, surely."

He turned away, moving back over to the horse. "You were betrothed the moment that you agreed to come with me."

Oh. Now that felt very serious, and I finally got the courage to ask. "My, um, betrothed – does he have the gift?"

"You don't want to know his name?"

"And his name," I added, but several seconds too late. "Tell me whatever you know."

Damon paused. "His name is Kajus," – he pronounced it like Kay-joos – "and he is both my cousin and a good man. He will be nineteen next winter, and he does have the gift. As for what form it takes…"

A little older than me, then. "Yes?"

"You'll have to see it for yourself."

Now that made me more nervous than anything else. From the reports I'd read about the Veest, they could turn into a whole range of creatures from eagles to wolves, pigs and bears – the last I'd just seen in person, of course. What could be so complicated about my betrothed's form that Damon couldn't explain it in one sentence?

I pondered the question while we rode along a tree-lined path, well-trod but increasingly green and thick with undergrowth. I could hear things moving about in the forest; shuffling sounds that I knew had nothing to do with our own movements, and it took a real effort not to react. *They're just people. No matter what they look like, they're just people…*

"So I heard that some Veest can hold a form halfway between animal and human," I said eventually. "Is that true?"

Damon paused a moment before answering. "It is. It's considered a sign of great strength to be able to do so for any length of time. It's good that you know this – you'll probably be met by some in such forms once we reach Veestlun."

"Veestlun? Is that…"

"Home of the gifted. Our city."

We wound our way around the steep sides of green hills and then down into a wide, curving valley, following alongside a small creek that turned into a substantial river. I heard the city before we reached it, those sounds of many people living all alongside each other reminding me of our old home. Perhaps no matter what language people spoke, no matter how they looked, once all together there was a similar sound, a similar feel. I hadn't been inside a large city in several years, but the memories lingered in my mind.

Where the cities of Enoria had been built of sun-bleached, golden sandstone, Veestlun was made of palest grey granite mottled with darker streaks, likely quarried directly from the surrounding hills. But where Enoria had been dry, this place was lush green. Green outside, green growing *up* the walls in the form of moss, green inside the city from trees planted in the streets, from pots lining windows and full of herbs.

People turned and watched us curiously, and I tried not to be too obvious about watching back. They were as I'd expected, somewhat paler than my people, although most weren't as milk-white as Damon. Most wore simple clothing in shades of green or pale yellow, so again, likely from what dyes were available around them. Most of their heads were topped with hair somewhere between mid-brown and what looked like actual gold, pretty enough to make me take a second glance, although I saw a few with Enorian-dark hair too.

Damon had been so vague about actual numbers that I almost expected to see animals roaming the streets, or sitting outside alehouses having dinner. But I could just see people, hundreds and hundreds of people, and the only animals I noticed were chickens pecking around in the dirt, hopping out of the way to avoid our horse's hooves. I did spot one large brown wolf trotting alongside a small child (although that could have been just a dog), a flash of huge pale wings on a distant rooftop, and yet another big brown bear, this time dragging in a bloodied carcass of what might have been a cow. I figured that the Veest knew who was their own, and who wasn't – or else they really *would* be cannibals.

As if guessing what I was thinking, Damon leaned forward and murmured, "Veest never turn into cows, or sheep, or any animal that chews the cud. The gift usually takes predator form."

I swallowed. And that was why my people were so afraid of his. "Good to know."

I saw my first animal-headed Veest just as we turned into the large courtyard of a building that seemed quieter than the rest, with only a couple of people moving in and out. At a small table nearby two Veest played what looked like chess, except one of the players wasn't moving the pieces with their hands. They – it – was sitting with its grey arms folded neatly, and an enormous wrinkly grey hose-thing hung down from its face and gently picked up the pieces, moving them from location to location. It also had huge flapping ears almost the size of dinner plates, and I gave up on my attempt to look unimpressed. I stared.

The Veest looked up from his game and stared back, looking past me to my companion. "Hi, Damon."

"Hi, Dasha. Who's winning?"

"Me, of course." The Veest – and it was a female if I judged that voice correctly – triumphantly moved another piece, and the human male sitting opposite her swore.

"What was she?" I asked in awe once we'd moved out of hearing range.

"Elephant," he replied succinctly. "And be aware, her hearing is excellent."

"Oh." I hadn't said anything bad, surely? But I decided then to not say anything at all if I could help it. An *elephant,* whatever that was. Not pretty, and apparently showing off her 'strength' by staying in half-shifted form.

We rode through an inner set of gates and if I hadn't guessed that we were somewhere important before, I did now. All around us were people in action, moving purposefully about the multiple levels of the large stone building. We dismounted and I was led down a series of halls by a mostly silent Damon, my own nervousness growing with every step until finally we reached a door all on its own. It was small and plain, but Damon barely paused, taking the key that hung on the nearby hook and unlocking it. He opened the door just enough for me to see a couch and a rug, and a window opposite looking out over the city. "Just in here. I'll let my uncle know we've arrived."

I stepped inside and that was when I saw my father, sitting at a desk with a long scroll unrolled in front of him and an ink-dipped quill in one raised hand. "Claire?"

"Father!" I ran forward and into his embrace, noting with relief that he seemed quite well-fed. That was a good sign, right? But his usually clean-shaven face was covered in a short grey beard, and I recognised his clothing as the same he'd worn when he left a month earlier. At least it looked as though it had been cleaned. "Are you well?"

"Well enough." He stepped back to look me up and down. "You look well too, my dear, although I must say I'm a little sorry to see you here. But I thought if it was anyone, it'd be you."

"But the letter…" I stared at him in amazement. "Didn't you write that if one of us didn't come to marry a Veest, then you'd not be allowed to leave?"

"Ah, yes." He looked away awkwardly. "That is unfortunately true, but I would never sacrifice one of your lives for my own. I've been quite well kept here, although they don't seem to understand the concept of shaving."

I lifted a hand to his scruffy cheek, and the hair was as short and prickly as I'd expected. I felt my eyes sting with unshed tears. "Why did you think it would be me?" I asked quietly. Was I expendable as Damon had said?

Father set his hand over mine, and in that moment I could see only affection in his expression. "Because you're the bravest," he replied, sounding a little surprised. "And because you love me. I'd hardly expect any of the other girls to do it."

"Oh." Was I the bravest, really? I felt my mood perk up a little, remembering how terrified Tabitha had been, and how everyone had regarded me as I'd left. Perhaps not so expendable after all. "Amadine would have done it," I had to say. "She liked the idea of wedding cake, and getting to wear a white dress."

Father made a scoffing noise that perfectly summed up how I'd also reacted. "That girl," he said fondly. "One day we'll make sure she gets a wedding cake of her own, but not for many years, I would hope. Now as for you, Claire, I was just looking over the contract that would be used...*will* be used... if you decide to go through with this."

He glanced over to the door, seemed to note that it was still open, then strode over to close it. In a much lower tone he said, "I won't blame you if you don't want to, my darling. They're not bad people – not like some I've met – but they're not the same as us, even if they are in human form. My little girl..."

I barely held back rolling my eyes. I might be short, but I hadn't been his little girl since Mother died six years ago, and I'd stepped in to run the house (or tent, rather). "The emissary said that with the treaty we could settle properly in Rose Valley, without fear of being attacked any further," I replied softly. "Do you think that they'll change their minds?"

Father opened his mouth, then closed it again. "Not as long as we don't change ours, I don't think."

I nodded thoughtfully, taking another look around me. As a whole, the room was certainly as nice or better than what we'd had back at the tent city. The bed was small but covered in a colourful quilt, and through a narrow doorway into a small connecting chamber I saw what had to be a garderobe.

A small shelf on the wall held a neat glazed vase containing a single yellow rose. It looked like the one Father had pressed into the letter, only rather less squashed, and it reminded me again of why we were here. "I didn't miss that you'd been locked in," I said quietly.

"More from principle than any attempt to restrain me," he replied just as quietly. "Even if I got out of this building, how would I get through the city unseen? They've kept me in my usual clothes for a reason. No one else here wears brown."

Just then there came a sharp tap on the door followed by, "Meal's ready," in a female, Veest-accented voice; the vowels short and clipped in contrast to our slower speech.

Father just about leapt forward. "Missus Babic's brought the evening meal."

She proved to be a tall, formidable-looking woman in her late forties, pale as they all were, but I didn't miss the admiring glance that my father gave her. That made me feel more secure than anything he'd said. I was following his lead in the way he responded to our – what, hosts? Captors? – and in spite of anything he'd said about our differences, he treated her with as much polite deference as he would any woman back home. She'd brought enough food for two, some kind of vegetable stew with rather tough bread, and we were left alone to eat it.

"You have to dip the bread until it softens," Father told me once he saw me gnawing at the lump. "They use it to scrape out the bowl."

I gave it a go, and it was far more edible that way, but I wasn't yet halfway through my serving when the door abruptly swung open. Now they hadn't locked it, but they also hadn't bothered to knock first. I turned to see who'd come in, and my piece of bread fell right into my bowl from my slack fingers.

I thought the elephant lady had been strange, but this was…I didn't even know. The *thing* was big, probably bigger than my father and he wasn't short, and it wore neat dark blue clothing in what looked to be expensive cloth, edged in fine gold embroidery. Black hair, very blue eyes, but that was the kind description.

I'll say 'he' from now on, since a female wouldn't have worn breeches, right? *He* was covered in thick black fur from his head to the tips of his ungloved fingers, and two large, pointed ears stuck right out the top of his head, almost like a puppy I'd once had. But that was where the dog resemblance ended. He had a wide, flat black snout with a curling white tusk coming from each side, and those bright blue eyes blinked at me from amongst all that dark fur. A dog...pig... man-thing. Then it spoke, its voice as rough as its appearance. "What, you're still eating?"

I finally managed to close my mouth, but I couldn't say anything. I looked across at my father, who seemed more rueful than horrified. "We've only just had the food delivered," he said politely. "Has your father called for us?"

The dog-pig-man grunted. Not like a pig, but like an impolite boy. "He told me to bring you to him. I can give you another ten minutes, but no longer."

Father looked at me. "You can finish, Claire." To the Veest he added, "This is my eldest. She's seventeen."

There was a brief silence where I just sat there with my half-full bowl of food, trying to figure out what to say. When Damon had told me not to react, I hadn't pictured *this*. "Nice to meet you," I said finally.

The Veest blinked at me. "You look younger."

"I get that a lot." But there were worse things than looking young.

There was a silence where I wondered if I should comment on *his* looks, but didn't dare. Then he nodded briefly and turned to leave. "I'll be back." He left as abruptly as he'd come in, and just before he vanished from sight I noticed the curling black tail sticking out from a neatly-cut hole in his breeches.

Once the sound of his footsteps faded, I couldn't hold in my reaction any longer. "Oh, my-"

Father reached across and slapped his hand across my mouth, just like Tabitha had done yesterday to Amadine. *He can hear you*, he mouthed out, lowering his hand. *Don't say anything unkind.*

I swallowed back the explosion of words that wanted to burst forth. The elephant woman had been weird, but this was a whole new level of ugly – scary-ugly. "I never got his name," I said finally.

Father was still watching me seriously, and now I saw pity in his expression. "Kajus," he replied. "His name is Kajus."

Kajus.

"Oh," I said weakly. "Kanut's son." I pushed away my bowl of stew, my appetite abruptly gone. So *that* was my betrothed. And he chose that form to meet me for the first time? He clearly didn't know anything about human girls, because he was lucky I hadn't screamed and thrown my bowl at him…or taken Missus Streeth's advice about the best places to land a punch.

Father nodded, and he leaned forward, his voice barely a whisper. "I won't blame you if you change your mind now you've seen what you're in for. I'll find some way out of this that doesn't involve you."

So I'd insult the Veest by turning down their ruler's son because he was too ugly. Way, way, *way* too ugly. "Don't be silly," I replied, just as quietly. "I'm sure he doesn't always look like that. He had…he had pretty eyes." He just needed to be smart and actually show his human form, thank you very much.

"Pretty eyes." Father shook his head in disbelief. "Keep that attitude, darling. You'll need it."

I would keep that attitude, I told myself stubbornly as we followed my beastly betrothed down the stone halls of the building. Heavens, his tail even wagged from side to side as we walked, and I couldn't take my eyes off it. It was like a dream – the dog-pig-man was to marry me, and he was even wearing boots…

But that was his Veest form, I reminded myself over and over. They could look like humans, he just hadn't chosen to do so right now because he was showing off, and he was probably not at all ugly once he'd changed. He had darker hair too than most Veest, and that pleased me. Although even an ugly, pale human would be a hundred times more appealing than *this*.

We stopped abruptly enough that I almost ran into Kajus's back. We were now in front of a set of large wooden doors, set in the same granite everything else was built of. Kajus gave them a sharp knock, then a gruff voice called, "Enter."

I'd thought it would be just one person – maybe a grey-furred version of his son – but inside was a whole room full of people, all sitting around a huge wooden table. Father was directed to the closest seat, and I stood behind him a little awkwardly. Kajus moved silently around to stand behind the man at the table's head. And he was just a man; one with a thick grey beard plaited with blue beads and eyes of the same colour, and he wore dark red, something I hadn't seen on anyone else. I even checked. There were several others in blue, a number in grey or green, but only one wearing red. Only one in Veest form, too, and that was my betrothed.

Kanut studied me across the long table even as I studied him, and I finally looked down, not wanting to be rude. "So you'd be the brave girl who wants to marry my son."

Hardly when he looked like *that*. "I want peace," I said when it became clear I was supposed to respond. "Peace, and a place for my people to settle and thrive. My father wouldn't have written such a letter unless he thought this was a safe place for me to live."

"Hmm." Kanut studied me again. "You're just a wee, soft thing. Alden said you were sixteen."

"Seventeen," I corrected patiently. "I'll be eighteen in summer."

"Gracious," I heard someone mutter. "Do they all grow

so tiny?"

I heard my father make a displeased sound, so I quickly cut in, "People come in all shapes and sizes."

The Veest ruler shrugged, waving a hand towards the murmuring room. "Well do we know that, little Claire. And if you lack stature, then your courage seems sufficient. So do you stand before us of your own free will to wed my son Kajus of Veestlun, not coerced by any of those back at your home, or even by Alden here?"

"I'm here of my free will," I replied calmly, although I felt anything but calm on the inside.

Kanut looked over his shoulder to his beastly son. "Kajus, do you stand here of your own free will to marry Claire the Enorian, not coerced by any other person?"

My betrothed paused only briefly. "I'm here of my own free will," he replied gruffly.

"Well. Good. Alden, man, you sign the betrothal contract, and we'll have you up and off by day's end," Kanut told my father, the conversation apparently done. "You can begin settling the upper valley within a month."

"We could be there within a week if needs be," my father replied. "Planting season's almost over. I know we'd appreciate the extra time."

The others at the table had largely been silent until now, but now a blue-clad fair-haired woman called out angrily, "You'll take what you're offered, human! This treaty is based on our kindness, nothing more!"

"And my willingness to give up my daughter," Father replied, his jaw tight. "Why not allow what will cause you no harm?"

"There are some living within the valley now," Kanut said. "They need time to leave."

"Oh." Father wouldn't argue with that, and it was clear he hadn't known. "Of course."

"But we will speak of this further," the Veest leader added. "Kajus, take your betrothed and show her the gardens while it is still light."

His betrothed. Argh, that meant *me*. But I followed him out, and the door hadn't even closed when I heard arguments burst out from within the room, and I looked back anxiously.

"It's the way they come to decisions," Kajus said, barely looking over his shoulder at me. "Don't worry for your father."

"Was I that obvious?"

One corner of that pig-like mouth curled into what might have been a smile. "I can smell your fear."

Now *that* scared me, and I stopped short. "Really?"

"No, of course not. Don't be silly, I'm not a dog."

"Oh. Of course." I followed his too-long steps along the hall, skipping to catch up as he reached an exit to an outer hall. The aforementioned gardens were close enough that I could smell them. "Um, if you don't mind me asking, what are you?"

"I'm a Veest."

"Yes, I know," I said, and I could hear a little of my agitation in my tone. "I had noticed that. What kind of animal do you change into?"

There was a long pause, then he replied, "I believe that my grandfather could turn into both a wolf and a boar. It was quite a gift."

"And you can take both forms at once." I struggled to find a nice comment to make. "That must mean you're very... powerful, right?"

Kajus laughed gruffly, and I suddenly realised that his tone wasn't necessarily from anger, but from the way his oddly-shaped mouth kept him from speaking normally. "Powerful? You could say that. Most people don't, though."

"What do they say?"

He turned away, one pointed ear twitching slightly. "They say I'm cursed."

With those odd words he took a long stride forward onto a leaf-covered path. There were fruit trees on either side of us, an orchard within a city; and I struggled to keep up in the receding light. My heart skipped a little in fear at being alone with him in this new place, but I set my trust in the thought that his character wasn't like his looks. He didn't *seem* beastly, not yet, anyway. "Because you can take both forms at once?" I asked again once I caught up. "How is it different from what Dasha did?"

"The difference," Kajus said grimly, "is that Dasha can turn back."

My breath stopped. "What?"

He was watching me, those bright blue eyes seeming so wrong in that black-furred face, and he was smiling a little. "I can't turn back, Enorian."

"I don't understand." Or maybe I did, but I didn't want to understand. Why was he smiling? "Is this a joke?"

He shook his head. "No. No, the joke is you turning up here and thinking you can live happily ever after with someone like *me*. You can barely stand to look at me, can you? And now we're legally joined. Lucky, lucky us."

I quickly diverted my gaze from his shirt front to his... face, if you could call it that, and it took real effort not to look away again. If an animal had a face like that, it'd be bearable. On a person, it was horrible. On my betrothed... "I've never seen anyone who looks like you," I said instead. "You've got to give me some time to get used to it. I mean, after we're married, when you take your human form-"

"Haven't you been listening to what I just said?" he shouted. "I don't have a human form anymore! I haven't in years!" And while I was taking that in, he added, "And we're legally betrothed, and that's as good as married to us! What did you think that was back in that room, idle questioning?"

I was so stunned that the information was sinking in very slowly. We were legally bound, and he would *always* look like that...? Oh, stars above... "But there was no ceremony," I said weakly. "No celebration." I thought of what Amadine had said. "Not even a cake."

"The celebration," Kajus said acidly, "comes with the birth of the first child. Do you know *anything* about the Veest?"

Birth of the first child? Oh, stars above… I felt my eyes sting, and something warm ran down my face. But the tears made me feel angry too. "No, I don't!" I snapped back. "I don't know, because this time last night I was only deciding to leave my home because I didn't want my father to die here, or my people to be pushed out of the first half-decent place we've found in years! And if you Veest knew anything about regular humans, you'd know that we don't change forms, and we don't have fur! We *do* have wedding celebrations, and no one gets married by mistake! You can't just spring something like this on me! It's not fair!"

When I'd finally run out of steam my 'husband' and I just stood there, staring at each other for long moments in dismay. Not a good start, and I still couldn't accept that he didn't change. "Why don't you have a human form?" I said finally, my voice cracking. "Why *you*?"

Why did you have to be the one to marry me, was the unspoken question, and he answered it grimly. "One day five years ago I changed forms, just as a game amongst friends, but I couldn't change back. Such things happen once in a hundred years. We don't choose it. As for why I'm to marry you – it's because my father told me to. I didn't choose *you* either, little girl. But here we are, for the sake of peace and our fathers. Or shall we tell them that we can't do it because I'm just too ugly for you, and you're too silly and weak for me…?"

Yes. Oh, *yes* he was too ugly. Too monstrous, more like it – as beastly in appearance as Tabitha had said the Veest were. I guessed she wasn't so silly after all.

3
The Tragedy

He couldn't change form. My betrothed couldn't change out of that horrible, hairy, beastly pig-wolf form. It was an absolute tragedy; the worst news I could have imagined.

But I couldn't pull out now. It would be a terrible insult to the Veest, and would shatter the fragile peace that this marriage was supposed to bring our people. Besides, silly and weak? No way!

"You said we were legally bound," I said instead, fixing my gaze on a nearby orange tree, its leaves seeming almost black in the growing darkness. "We can't break it off."

"Do you feel legally bound? Because I don't."

Just like the comment about not celebrating until the birth of the first child, that made me feel incredibly uncomfortable. I wasn't prudish, or at least I didn't think I was. I mean, I wouldn't exactly know, since I was only seventeen and with only fifty people in our village, there weren't a lot of chances for suitors. But when I'd thought of suitors, and of husbands, the blurry image in my head hadn't been anything near *this*.

"We've only just met," I replied in a low voice. "Of course I don't feel bound. I feel like this is some sort of joke, like people are waiting for this to go wrong so they can laugh, maybe, or start a war. But I'll tell you what, I am *not* going to give up on this. Not this quickly, and not because you've got a hairy pig-face and I *really* wasn't expecting that."

Oops, I hadn't meant to say that aloud. He obviously hadn't expected to hear it either, because he was visibly taken back. Then he retorted, "Well, I wasn't expecting a soft, stuck-up little foreign girl, but then I guess a hairy pig-faced Veest can't be too fussy, can he? I'll consider myself lucky that you haven't run off to throw up in the bushes."

No, but if he wanted to kiss me then I'd probably end up gagging. I took a deep, calming breath, turning away to walk further down the path as a sort of distraction. I could smell the scent of roses in the air, but I couldn't see any in this dim light. "I'm sorry I said that."

"But you meant it," he called after me.

True. I stopped, turning back to face him. "But I didn't mean to *say* it, because it was unkind."

"So what, am I supposed to apologise for what I said?"

I sighed. "Whatever. I don't care. So what are we supposed to be doing out here besides arguing?"

"Traditionally couples spend some quiet time together in the bower over there, then spend the night getting to know each other. But we'll pass on that, shall we?"

I desperately, desperately wanted to be out of his presence, to finish this awkward 'meeting'. But I wasn't stupid. "Then we'll spend the night. Maybe we can talk."

I marched resolutely forward and found the entrance to the bower. Inside was a large room, lit gently with a couple of torches in the walls, and filled with the scent of the surrounding fruit trees. Piles of cushions were scattered over the stone floor. Someone had even put down a flask of drink and a plate of something chocolatey, proof that the Veest weren't entirely barbarians. It would have been romantic if I'd been here with, say, Alec. *Who probably also thinks I'm a too-soft, stuck up little girl,* I reminded myself. But I wasn't betrothed to *him*, was I? More was the pity.

I sat with a plunk next to the chocolates and poured myself a drink. It was reddish purple and reminded me a little of grape juice, although it tasted a little sour. Not bad, though. "Do you want one?" *You big, rude, hairy, pig-faced person.*

He just stood there for a moment, eyes almost glowing in the torches' reflected light, then shook his head. "No."

"Fine," I replied tersely, taking a large gulp. "Suit yourself."

The silence stretched out long enough to become awkward, then he said abruptly, "I'm going for a walk."

And off he went, leaving me with the wine and the chocolate, and the space to get really, really upset over what had just happened.

Yes, I cried. Quite a lot, actually; wouldn't you if you found out that your sort-of-husband was about as bad as you could have imagined? OK, so he hadn't beaten me or even shouted, but he was, as kindly as I can put it, not human. If I was to be unkind I'd say he was a monster, and we were almost married. The celebration came after the birth of the first child...and they'd already given us a room together. It seemed that the Veest had a different idea of betrothals than we did, even past the lack of celebration.

"I didn't ask for this," I said tearfully to no one in particular, and into the silence another thought popped into my head.

Neither did he.

Yes, well, of course Kajus had already said that he'd been told to marry me. That was no surprise...

But then the image came to mind of a boy, perhaps dark-haired and blue-eyed, looking into the mirror one morning and finding that who he'd once been was now gone, replaced by something that only a mother could love – or maybe not even then. So I was stuck, apparently married to a really 'gifted' Veest, but he had to live inside that body *all* the time.

That made me think. See, there were all sorts of causes for curses: family feuds, getting on the wrong side of a power-user, or even just breaking a mirror (or so people said). But just as often there were ways to break curses, each one tailored to that particular curse. Or so I had read. Apparently there were even Wyse folk who spent their time going around breaking curses, like travelling do-gooders.

So surely all curses could be broken?

With that hope I said a little prayer, as I sat alone in that fruit-scented room. I prayed that if there was a way out of this, a way to make things right for Kajus and for my people, that we'd find it. And I couldn't say that I felt better, or that I had any answer right then and there, but the situation I was in felt just a little less terrible.

I woke up in the early hours to find the room barely lit from moonlight through the partially-covered windows. On the far side of the room, amongst a pile of cushions, was a large dark shape, its back to me. From here he could almost be any boy I knew, dark-haired and lanky. But the daylight would tell the truth. So I repeated that little prayer silently to myself, and went back to sleep.

By morning I was alone again, and the sun was streaming in through the gaps in the curtains. Someone was banging a drum right next to my head, the sound echoing horribly, and I groaned.

"Time to get up!" someone shrieked. "Even new brides can't mope around in bed all day!"

New bride? Who? Oh, they meant *me*...and thank heavens that wasn't true in the most technical sense. The girl who'd been sent to wake me bustled around too noisily for a bit, then finally, blessedly left. I dozed a little longer, my head still aching, and then finally forced myself to get up.

After dressing, I saw there were two little notes tacked up by the doorway. One read, *Claire, I had to return to our people to give them the good news. I expect to see you again very soon. With love, Father.*

Oh. Father had gone, and without saying goodbye? I pushed back the sudden sense of abandonment, knowing there must have been a good reason that he did so. And I *would* see him again.

But the second, even shorter note was in a different hand, with a distinctively non-Enorian flourish. It read, *Find*

Cassiana. She'll give you your duties.

Not a single mention of our betrothal-marriage-thingy, but duties? I had duties? But I'd had them back at home too, I reminded myself, although there was plenty of time to rest as well. Still, it was with some nervousness that I took my tidier self back to the main building, feeling slightly better but still not my best. Either that food had disagreed with me, or else that drink had been more alcoholic than I'd thought.

It turned out to be the second. "Drink too much blackberry wine and you'll sleep all day," Cassiana told me condescendingly. I'd been directed to her pretty much straight away; a girl of my own age pressing linen in a high-roofed, light-filled room. The sun had come through the window and turned her hair into bright gold, and even in my hungover state I was a little dazzled.

Cassiana, AKA Cass, was tall, willowy and beautiful in a very pale sort of way, and I began to realize that I wasn't just small, soft and sun-browned by my people's standards, but by his even more so. And she didn't even have to be bejewelled to look good – she wore only a simple gold globe medallion around her white neck.

I don't care, I told myself, *and I won't be intimidated.* "I didn't realize it was alcoholic," I said calmly. "I won't make that mistake again."

Cass gave me a derisive glance. "You're not used to a little wine, cutie? How old are you?"

"Seventeen," I said for what felt like the hundredth time. Cutie, was I? I guessed that would make her Beauty. "How old are you?"

She flicked her hair, and it poured silkily over her shoulder, catching the sun again. That had to be intentional. "Nineteen next winter. On the same day as your husband, actually."

"Oh? When's that?" May as well know when his birthday was, if nothing else.

"Are you just going to watch me?" she snapped suddenly. "Start folding the ironed sheets." Then in a gentler tone she

35

added, "The 26th day of Pasture Month. An auspicious day for the Veest. Children born then are considered to be very blessed. Strong, intelligent, beautiful."

I'd followed her instructions with the sheets, but I was disliking her more with every word. "And are you?"

"Am I what?"

"Considered to be *blessed*." Kajus sure wasn't, based on what he'd just told me.

Cass lifted her chin, sliding the heated iron quickly across someone's embroidered jacket. "Kajus always told me that I was, even though I don't have the gift. But that was before…"

I knew she was prompting me, but I answered anyway. "Before what?"

"Before I said something very foolish, something that hurt him. See, before he changed, he was sweet on me." She shrugged prettily. "He was handsome enough, although rather dark for a Veest, like his mother had been. Not as dark as you, of course. But he's so sensitive! I made some foolish remark about his looks, and he never forgot it. Not once, and it's never been the same since."

Naturally he'd be sweet on her. I hadn't seen that many Veest, but I could guess that most of them didn't look like this one. But it would be a terrible match with Kajus the way he was now – Beauty and the beast. I couldn't just take her words as kindly meant, though. I didn't know what she'd said to him that had offended him so much, but I'd called him a hairy pig-face. Very accurate, but if he held grudges, then how could he forget *that*? "Considering that I'm the one marrying him," I said calmly, "that's a useful thing for me to know. I'll watch my words."

"Hmm." Cass finished the jacket. "Hang this up to cool. If it creases again, you'll be the one re-ironing it."

"You know, you can ask me rather than ordering," I said mildly. "If we're to be working together then we may as well get on."

"I thought I *was* asking," she replied, sounding surprised. "Hang the jacket, will you?"

I hung the jacket, then asked a question I'd been wondering for some time, ever since we'd arrived in this area and had discovered the locals weren't precisely…normal. "So what's the point of the Veest gift, anyway?"

Cass stopped halfway through spreading out a thin white cloth. "Excuse me?"

Had I said the wrong thing? But in spite of her reaction, I persisted. "You know. The whole turning-into-animals thing. You can't do it, and neither can Damon. But Dasha and Kajus can, obviously. But…" I paused, trying to think of the best way to say it. "…but what can people do in animal form that they can't do as human? What's the advantage of it besides showing, um, strength?"

She finished spreading out the cloth on the ironing board, then picked up the hot iron, holding her hand near the metal to test the heat. "You mean that Veest can't iron in animal form. They can't cook, they can't sew or farm or even have a proper conversation. Being fully changed means their thought processes are different too, so they can't be trusted to act as they normally would. Sure, a bear or a wolf can go hunting, but they'll bring the catch back in a real mess. A hunter with arrows can do just the same thing!"

Her tone had become heated, and I felt my eyebrows raise. I hadn't expected such a strong reaction, and it seemed like she was voicing my own thoughts. "I hear some Veest can turn into birds," I ventured. "It would be really useful to see the world from a height. It would help in…" *battle*, I almost said, then remembered what we were trying to avoid. "…Um. All sorts of things, I imagine."

There was a silence broken by the faint hiss of the iron on the damp fabric. Then Cass said sweetly – so sweetly I knew she was regretting her outburst – "We Veest greatly value the gift and those who hold it. I wouldn't recommend insulting us again, especially in front of people who aren't as gracious as I am."

"I wasn't insulting-"

"And besides," she cut in, "all this chatter is distracting

me from my work. See, I've marked the cloth! Now hush, and let's focus."

I studied her for a few moments, but her attention seemed fully on the movement of the iron. The conversation was clearly over, but my curiosity had been piqued.

The rest of the day was spent following Cass around, being taught the basic duties of a young woman here in the large building they called 'the castle'. (Although it wasn't my idea of a traditional castle, as it was inside the city walls rather than a fortress of its own.) My duties mostly involved menial tasks, cleaning, cooking and tidying on an industrial scale: nothing new, nothing horrible.

"When you have children then your duties will change," Cass told me later in the day as we peeled vegetables, glancing at me slyly under her eyelashes. "Do you think that will be soon?"

Only if the father wasn't Kajus. "I couldn't say," I retorted coolly. "How about you? Do you have a suitor?"

She looked away. "I did, but he was recently betrothed to someone else."

She must mean Kajus, but she'd earlier said he was annoyed at her about something. I could definitely understand that emotion. But if I believed her, then Kajus was still courting her regardless of any grudge. I bit back the sudden feeling of insecurity and resolved to ask him – if I could ever get him to stop long enough to talk. "I'm sorry to hear that."

"Not that sorry, or you'd break it off and go home," Cass said lightly, still not meeting my eyes. "But perhaps I'm asking too much. You *are* to be the wife of the son of Veestlun's ruler. Quite a high position."

I stopped what I was doing, turning to stare at her. There were too many things wrong in that statement to address all at once, but, "You'd marry him as he is now?" I asked bluntly. "I find that hard to believe."

She lifted her chin again. "Just because *you* find him

hideous, doesn't mean everyone does."

"I didn't say-"

"Never mind what you *said*. Anyway, you don't know much about Veest, or you'd know that gifted ones like him don't have to stay that way."

My heart skipped a beat. "He can change?"

"Only," Cass said deliberately, "if he finds someone he wants to change for enough to break the gift's power." She put down the small knife she'd been peeling with. "Do you think he'll want to change for *you*, Claire?"

No. The answer was no, Kajus did not want to change for me. He didn't even want to talk to me. After the first night I'd been moved into a room in the main building, one with a double bed and a wardrobe, and a big rug in front of the fire.

Unsurprisingly, Kajus slept on the rug. I thought it was less a 'dog' thing and more trying to avoid me, and I had the usual mixed reaction of both relief and dismay. I did *not* want him to be my real husband, but I really, really didn't want the sort-of marriage broken off and the peace treaty annulled. Better to have never had a treaty at all than to have it ruined by insult.

But seriously, I told myself as I furiously cleaned clothing on a wooden washboard, ignoring the other young women chattering around me. Out of all the Veest here, they picked the one who didn't have a human form? And then back when I'd agreed to marry him, they'd acted all offended when Father tried to change the settlement dates by even a week, like they'd done us a real favour. They kind of had, but it was at a high price. It was like they *wanted* me to run off screaming so they'd have a reason to attack our people...

Oh, stars above. I dropped the wet cloth right into the soapy water, sucking in a breath as I realised the truth of that thought. Of *course* they wanted an excuse to make war – or some of them did, at least. If I was to react badly, to reject Kajus and the marriage as it would be so easy to do, then that would be the kind of insult that could spark all-out battle, and we would lose.

Badly.

That wasn't an option, I resolved as I found the cloth and began scrubbing with renewed determination. I would never give such an insult. I would be kind and wifely and…I didn't know, all the things that would make the Veest think well of me, and of my people. And maybe, just maybe, that would make Kajus want to change for me. Or if he didn't, I would go find a handy Wyse person to help me along.

That evening at dinner I had the opportunity to eat with all the other young women as I had for the last two nights. I looked across the room and saw amongst those human faces a single black-furred one, sitting alone in the corner, focused on some wrinkled papers in front of him. There was an empty space beside him, so I ladled some stew into my purple-edged wooden bowl, then moved to take the seat. I heard the noise in the hall quieten slightly as I did, then pick up again as if people were pretending they hadn't noticed.

Kajus jolted in surprise, then raised his eyebrows. "The women's table's over there."

"Mm, but I haven't seen you in a while," I replied with a smile, sitting down anyway. "Besides, it's not compulsory to sit with the women, is it?"

"I'm reading," he said deliberately.

"Great, I love to read. Maybe you can pass me the pages when you're done with them."

He raised a hairy eyebrow disbelievingly. "Sure, you'd want to read the latest reports on the cold war between Sudante and East Arland. All girls love that kind of thing."

"Actually, the cold war is between Sudante and West Arland, but I can understand why you made that mistake. They're both in the Summer Sea, and both don't seem to understand how to get on with their neighbours." At his surprised expression I added casually, "I read the reports after my father's done with them. Very interesting."

He paused. "And you'd know about getting on with your neighbours…?"

If that was a dig at my people in general or at me personally, I ignored it. "I'm not perfect, but hopefully I can learn from my mistakes. But my dinner's getting cold. Can I read that first page if you're done with it?"

Kajus passed me the page, and then we sat for the rest of the meal in silence, reading and eating and for the most part, trying to keep the stew off the reports. After the first few minutes I relaxed enough that I didn't have to pretend anymore, and I really did get caught up in what I was reading. These reports were basically political gossip, produced by travelling writers and passed along to anyone who had the money to buy them. "I wonder if these are even true," I mused aloud after a while. "Couldn't clever rulers pay to have the information warped for their own purposes?"

"They probably do," Kajus agreed. "But if you knew what sort of lies they'd tell, you might be able to guess the truth by reading between the lines."

"Oh? How do you mean?"

He paused, and then launched into an explanation that made me realise he'd actually thought this through, and if these were all his ideas he was actually quite intelligent. I listened in interest for some time, not really noticing the time passing until someone's hand tapped lightly on my shoulder.

It was Cass. "I hope you don't mind me butting in," she said cheerily, "but you look half asleep, Claire. Have you not been going to bed early enough?"

Kajus clammed up immediately, and I knew the implications of what was being said – or how he'd taken it, anyway. We hadn't been keeping each other up at night, so I must have been bored.

"I'm fine," I tried to say. "We were talking about-"

"Good to see you again, Kajus," Cass said warmly to my husband as though I hadn't spoken. "You're looking well. I suppose the betrothal must suit you."

That last was said with a longing note that I didn't miss, and didn't trust. I scowled at her, but Kajus's reaction had been quite different. He had blushed as much as a person covered in fur *could* blush (hint, it was in the expression rather than the colouring) and once he looked at her, he couldn't seem to look away.

"I'm well enough," he replied gruffly, standing abruptly and picking up his bowl. "I'll just return this to the kitchen. Claire, you can give me the report back when you're done with it."

Then he left, Cass turning to watch him go with a sigh. "Such a shame we don't talk anymore," she mused. "I hope I didn't cause any trouble. It's just I know he can get focused on these oddball subjects and it's hard to show him you aren't interested, you know?"

"Actually I was interested," I retorted. "And perhaps that's why you don't talk anymore, because he knows you think he's boring."

"I do *not* think he's boring," she said huffily. "I was trying to be helpful."

Sure she was. But that night, rather than going to bed as soon as possible to avoid Kajus, I waited up for him. He came in quietly and very late, and I'd almost dozed off on top of my book where it sat on a small side table, the candle burning low next to it.

"Why are you still up, Enorian?"

"I wanted to talk to you."

He came a little hesitantly into the room, setting down what looked like a longbow into the corner, and taking off his jacket. "If you must."

Restrain your enthusiasm, Kajus. "Have you been hunting?"

"In the dark? Of course not. I'm supposed to restring this before the competition tomorrow."

"Oh? I haven't heard about any competition."

"It's every year," he replied after a pause. "Strength, accuracy, wits. The final is weeks away, but the first archery test is tomorrow. I doubt you'll care about it."

"I'm actually not bad with a bow and arrow," I joked, but it fell flat. "I am interested, and I was interested in our conversation earlier, even if Cass made it seem otherwise."

Kajus turned away, focusing on rearranging the bow where it sat against the wall. "Why are you doing this?"

"Doing what?"

"Acting *interested,* as you put it. Are you afraid that I'll break it off and ruin the peace treaty?"

My heart sank. My motives weren't so hidden, it seemed, and his continued prickliness irked me. "Yes, yes I am. And I suppose that for you wonderful Veest, you can end a betrothal just as easily as you start one, is that right? Perhaps I'll turn around one day and find I said the wrong thing, and that'll be it. Done, and it'll somehow be my fault."

"No need to get snippy. I was asking an honest question."

"Honest question?" I cried out. "How's this for an honest question. Are you aware, oh husband, that your people want me to give up on this marriage so that they'll have a reason to attack mine? Because I can't think that you wouldn't have noticed!"

He made a sound of scorn. "Don't be stupid. Where did you get that idea?"

"Because I feel like nobody, least of all you, has made an effort to make this easy for me. And that thing with Cassiana-"

And now I actually saw his ears prick, even though he wasn't looking at me. Prick, like a dog's. "What about her?" he asked casually. "Did she say something about me?"

Too casual, and I wasn't fooled. I was tired from sleeplessness and from trying to fake being content over these last few days, as if I wasn't surrounded by unfamiliar things and unfamiliar people, and without friends. "She said that you were sweet on her, and that you were considered a suitor before I arrived."

Kajus went silent, finally stopping his distracted rearranging of his bow. "I wasn't a suitor," he said finally. "She'd never have considered me, and her family wouldn't have allowed it because of how I look. But I'm sure she's with Damon, even though her mother Daphne doesn't approve."

"Damon the emissary?" I said in surprise. I noted Kajus hadn't denied that he was sweet on her, though.

"Damon who brought you here," he agreed. "He does everything he can to impress Cass's mother, including taking the risk of going to your people, but I don't think it will matter. Daphne is a tanist, and she wants Cass to marry accordingly."

"Oh." I paused, thinking of pale, boyish Damon standing amongst my people, having just delivered the bad news of Father's capture. He hadn't seemed at all afraid, but Kajus was right. It *had* been a risk. "Er…what's a tanist?"

He looked at me for a moment, eyebrows raised as if testing whether I was joking, then seemed to realise my question was genuine. "Being a tanist means you could be the next ruler," he answered finally. "There are ten tanists in Veestlun, and one day when my father is very old – or just tired – he'll choose his heir from those ten. I'm a tanist. Damon isn't." His blue eyes narrowed. "Did you think I would be the next ruler, Claire? Because I'm Kanut's son? I hope you're not disappointed, because it'll probably never happen."

"I hadn't thought about it," I replied honestly. "There's been so much going on, I hadn't even made the connection that you could be the next ruler. And I don't mind if you won't be, because I don't really want to be a ruler's wife."

My eyes widened as I realised what I'd just said. Too honest, perhaps? So I quickly changed the subject. "Anyway, about Cass. She implied that you'd have married her if not for me, and maybe…maybe you would have been able to change back to human for her. Break the curse, I mean."

There was a very long, awkward silence, then at last he replied, his tone flat. "It's not true. Nothing can break this curse, or gift, whatever people call it. And with it I never would have been able to marry her, not in a hundred years. I'm not going to break it off with you, and my people don't want to rush in and murder all of yours, wherever you got that idea. I'd appreciate it if we stopped talking about this subject. I need to get an early night."

We were well past any chance of an early night, and I was feeling confused and perhaps a little ashamed. So much for wanting to make friends, because I'd done the exact opposite. His words had made me question what I'd thought, and perhaps it was my own loneliness and defensiveness that had made me take that attitude. I could see that he *was* sweet on Cass, but it was a sore spot with him.

He went into the small dressing chamber to get changed, and I got into bed. When he came back out I said very quietly, "I'm sorry for what I said. I've been scared, maybe, that I'd ruin everything here, and my family would suffer. I hope you can forgive me."

He was wearing a long dark blue nightrobe (dark blue was a theme, perhaps?) and he looked just as awkward as I felt. It was a strange thing, for two strangers to share a bed, to share a room without passion or even friendship. "Of course I can forgive you. Just stop trying so hard, alright? I promise that I won't break it off, not unless you do something dreadful. And anything that came before – we won't mention it."

"I won't try so hard if you won't actively avoid me. And what kind of dreadful things could you mean?"

Kajus looked at me, then looked away. "It usually involves unfaithfulness."

"There's not anybody I'm interested in. Besides, I was raised better than that." I'd keep to my vows, such as they were, until *he* changed his mind. Not me.

"Not even back amongst your people? A certain Arrick, perhaps?"

Arrick? Oh, *Alec.* "I'm guessing Damon mentioned Alec, though I've no idea how or why he'd have heard about him. But there's nothing between us." I tightened my lips, wondering how much to say. "He wasn't interested."

My sort-of-husband let out a soft laugh, the sound sitting oddly with his appearance. "Then perhaps we're two of a kind." He went to sit down on the thick fur rug in front of the dimming fire, grabbing the blanket that he'd folded off to the side.

On an impulse I said, "You don't have to sleep on the

floor. There's enough room up here."

He seemed to think it through. "Maybe some other time."

"Oh. OK. Good night, then."

"Good night."

I extinguished the candle, and then the room was dark; silent except for my breathing and his over the other side of the room. I wasn't tired anymore, so I just lay there and thought about what I'd found out today. No matter what he'd said, I wasn't convinced that some of the Veest wouldn't love an excuse to break our fragile truce. And as for not being able to break the gift/curse…perhaps that was a relief. I wasn't keeping him from freedom any more than he was keeping me from Alec. With or without this marriage, it wouldn't make any difference.

I must have slept, because I woke with a jolt sometime later, some unfamiliar sound breaking my rest. A moment later I realised it was Kajus. He was tossing and turning in his sleep, his form lit up faintly by the usual moonlight through the narrow gap in the curtains, so it was like I was seeing in black and white. For a moment his pig-like face twisted into a snarl, and then suddenly it blurred and changed, the fur melting away into an instant of beauty. But then he relaxed, and the usual wolf-pig had returned, just the same as always.

I caught my breath. Had I imagined it? But then a moment later it happened again, that twist of discomfort quickly followed by a complete change into pale skin, long black hair, and very human features. This time the change stayed, and I just stared, unable to take my eyes off him. "Stars in heaven," I breathed in amazement. "He *has* changed."

4
The Change

So much for Kajus saying he couldn't change. Yet here he was, asleep but most certainly in human form. My heart pounding with excitement, I crept out of bed, wanting a closer look but not wanting to wake him. I crouched down beside him on the rug, and that beautiful, hairless human form remained. In this dim light I could only see shades of grey, but I could make out the shape of his nose, cheekbones, lips…all where you'd expect them to be, and utterly, utterly miraculous on this boy.

He frowned in his sleep, flat eyebrows tenting into the centre of his brow, and I couldn't help myself. I had to prove this was real. I reached out to touch that smooth forehead, and as my fingertips made contact, suddenly the change reversed. Like a mask being put on, the black fur rushed back over his skin leaving only bare patches around his eyes, and his features distorted back into that extreme ugliness that I'd almost got used to. The disappointment was immense.

His eyes snapped open. "What are you doing?"

I was still sitting over Kajus, my hand barely touching his face. "You changed," I told him, my tone still showing my amazement, and perhaps a little defensive. "You changed into human form."

"What? I did not."

47

"You did," I insisted, still clinging to the memory of what I'd seen. "You had pale skin and long black hair. Just now."

He sat up, pushing my hand away. "I did not change, Enorian. I do not *change*. You had a dream. Now go back to sleep."

"I wasn't dreaming," I said in a low voice. "You must have been. What were you dreaming about? *Who?*" It surely wasn't me, not by the way he'd changed back once I'd touched him.

For a moment he seemed taken back, then shook his head. "Nothing and nobody. Now go back to bed, unless you're wanting company?"

I scuttled back quickly, shaking my head.

"I thought not."

"But you did change, Kajus," I told him again, this time from a safe distance. "You *did*."

He just rolled his eyes, barely visible in the dim light. "Good *night*, Enorian."

Was it a good night? But I knew what I'd seen, and I wasn't going to give up that easily.

Maybe I'd have to visit the Wyse people after all.

The first archery competition was the following day, and we were all freed from our duties long enough to watch from the windows and cheer the others on. There were about thirty competitors of all ages, even a few girls and milk-white Damon the emissary, but I didn't see Kajus anywhere.

I commented on it to Sala, one of the friendlier girls who I shared duties with, and she gave me an odd look. "Kajus doesn't compete in this competition. He's gifted."

"But I saw him…" Cleaning his bow, I almost said, but kept it to myself. "Do the gifted never compete at all?"

"They can only take part in most games in human form," she replied, eyes still fixed on the competitors below us. "They're too strong otherwise, and it's not an even contest. He can't take human form, so he doesn't compete. As I said."

He *can*, I thought to myself mutinously, even if he didn't

believe me. I hadn't been dreaming, and I knew what I'd seen. But it was a shame that he couldn't compete – it seemed that his 'gift' had kept him from a normal life in more than one way. "Does he hunt, then? Or isn't he allowed to use a bow at all?"

Sala seemed surprised that I'd asked. "Of course he's allowed to use a bow. He's Kanut's son, and a tanist. For now, at least."

Not good enough to compete, though. "What do you mean, for now?"

"Oh, you didn't know? Tanists must be able to lead in human form. If they're stuck as an animal for five years, then they lose their position. Kajus's time is up in...ooh, three months? Everyone knows about it, and that he'll never be chosen as ruler for that reason."

"Oh." Poor Kajus. I didn't care about position; in fact I'd be more comfortable being as ordinary as possible. But it seemed his 'gift' actually robbed him of a lot, even here in his home.

That evening I made a point to sit at Kajus's table before he could comment. "Don't say I'm trying too hard," I said quickly. "You've got my company, and you can't get away." He looked startled, so I added a bit more meekly, "Please don't walk away. It'll be embarrassing."

He made a surprised laugh. "Heaven forbid I embarrass you, Claire. Did you have a good day?"

Oh, a normal sort of question. "I cleaned, cooked, did a bit of sewing with the other girls. Very ordinary." And not at all thrilling. "I also watched the archery competition."

His eyes slid away from mine, smile faltering. "Ah. And you're wondering about the bow I restrung last night. It was for Damon – I'm told I'm quite good at that sort of thing."

"Good enough that you'll leave everyone else in the shade?" I asked teasingly.

Kajus looked flustered, then laughed. "Yes, of course. I'm purely brilliant, and that's why I can't be allowed to compete. It's just an old rule, Enorian, and one I don't care about."

49

"OK." But I didn't believe him. More than anything I wanted to bring up what had happened the night before, but somehow I managed to restrain myself. "Pass me the rest of the report when you're done."

We sat in companionable silence for a while until he'd finished eating. But he didn't get up to leave straight away. "So…do you have any memory of what happened last night?" he asked carefully. "Or were you actually sleep-walking and don't recall it?"

"What happened last night, eh?" one of the young men called ribaldly from a nearby table. "And she might have been sleeping? Bad form, Kajus!"

Some of the others laughed, and he scowled. "It seems like we can't have a single conversation in here that isn't interrupted."

I put down my bowl. "I'm pretty much done anyway. And I *do* want to talk about this."

We ended up going outside, back into the orchard where I'd first found out about his 'gift'. Less than a week had passed, but it felt like a lot longer.

It was a lovely evening, the surroundings were beautiful, and I didn't want to bring up subjects that could cause arguments. So instead I just enjoyed the fresh air, admiring the lush, healthy trees…and the occasional highly-scented rose bush, generously covered in yellow or pink blooms. I also spotted a familiar gnarled form amongst the fruit trees. "Oh, is this an Enorian oak? I didn't realise they grew here!"

"We call them harmony oaks," Kajus replied. He stepped up to the tree, setting one furred hand against its rough trunk. "If they like you, then arrows made from their wood will never miss their mark."

"Yep, sounds like an Enorian oak," I said, a small smile curling my lips. I set my hand against the rough bark, next to his. My skin was almost the colour of the bark, just more golden brown, and it looked small and almost childlike next to his. I let out a depressed sigh.

"What, the tree doesn't like you?"

I rolled my eyes, but didn't pull my hand away. "My people tend to be smaller than yours, you may have noticed. I'm especially small. I just feel kind of…dwarfish next to you. Everyone here, really."

"That's because you are dwarfish. An adorable miniature person." His eyebrows shot up. "Are you part dwarf?"

"No!" But my cheeks were heating at the compliment hidden in his words. Adorable, was I? It was a bit better than 'cute', even though I'd rather be beautiful. "Well… I might be. My mother was small like me, and *her* father was also really short." I shrugged. "Maybe there is a dwarf or two amongst my ancestors, although I'd be surprised. I hear that most dwarves keep to themselves." Most races didn't intermingle. I'd never heard of any half dwarves, or half trolls, or half winged Wyse folk.

Kajus was quiet for a moment. "Do you have any magic?"

"No, unfortunately." Because if I did, I'd break his curse in an instant. I asked a little more hesitantly, "Does my size bother you?"

He let out a harsh sound that I realised a moment later was laughter. "*You* are asking if *your* looks disturb me? Do you realise how foolish that is?"

I set my hands on my hips and glared up at him. "You won't think it's foolish when your curse is broken, and suddenly you're the eligible ruler's son who's being chased by all the girls, but who's tied to some short foreigner. So yes, I am asking."

His smile faded. "You really seem convinced, don't you? Last night I woke up to find you with your hand on my face, saying that I'd…changed. I was going to ask if you remembered, but it seems that you do."

"Of course I remember!" I retorted. "I wouldn't forget something like that, so yes, I am convinced that the curse can be broken. It can, and it was for a good fifteen seconds last night. Do you remember what you were dreaming about when I woke you? It looked disturbing."

Kajus turned away, flexing his hands as if his thoughts

51

agitated him. "I was being drowned in a bog, then suddenly I was back out in the fresh air, and it was so bright I couldn't see anything. And then I woke up and you were right there."

Oh. That wasn't what I'd expected. "You weren't dreaming about a certain person in particular?" Cass, for example?

He shook his head. "No. But Claire, I've shared a room for years. Up until last month I shared with Damon, and he never once said anything about me changing. And he would say, because he knows what it means for me. So after so long, I just find it hard to believe…"

"To believe *me*?" I watched his face, noting the small areas of pale skin right around his eyes and under his snout, echoed in the gaps between his padded fingers. That boy I'd seen was in there, somewhere. "I know that you don't really know me, but I'm not a liar, and I'm not fanciful, either. Just ask anyone who knows me."

He looked away. "I'm afraid that your family will run screaming when they see me. So I won't ask, if you don't mind."

"Don't be silly. My father didn't run, and neither did I." I reconsidered what he'd said. "What do you mean, *when?* Do we have a visit planned?"

"You didn't know? A party of your people has been invited to the tournament as part of the treaty and for the wedding celebrations. I don't know who's coming, though."

"But I thought Veest didn't celebrate weddings 'til…"

"After the first child?" Kajus shrugged. "My father must have been speaking with yours, because he said your people would expect a celebration up front, and he thought it was a good idea. I don't see the harm in it."

My people were coming to stay – and we were going to celebrate the 'wedding'. Argh. Suddenly I felt ill, and it was a few moments before I remembered what we'd been talking about. "But Kajus, the curse-"

"Please Claire, I don't want to talk about it anymore," he interrupted. "I can't bear false hope. If it happens, it happens, but if not…"

False hope, eh? I pressed my lips together, holding back the defensive words. "Fine. I won't bring it up again…not unless there's something I really know can help."

He scoffed. "We'll need a miracle, Enorian. Now do you want to show me how you use a bow and arrow? I might not be able to compete, but you could."

"I was kind of joking when I said I was a decent shot," I said half an hour later as yet another arrow went wide of the target. "In truth, I haven't shot an arrow in years. If this is how I'm shooting now, there's no way I'm going to stand up in front of everyone and do this."

Kajus, in spite of his initial positive attitude, seemed to agree. "Wait here." Then he suddenly strode off, disappearing into the orchard. He reappeared after a few minutes holding a wonky brown stick. "Here, try this."

I looked at the thing dubiously. "You're kidding me."

"It's harmony oak, Enorian. If you want it enough, it'll hit the target. We use this wood for hunting all the time."

He looked so sincere, but I rolled my eyes. "Yeah, hit it then fall off again. We use them for hunting too…or used to. We've still got a few arrows we brought from Enoria, and it's precious. But this isn't exactly pointed, Kajus. It has to *stick*."

"Very well." He took back the stick, then pulling a knife from his belt, proceeded to quickly whittle its end into a rough point, and to smooth off the most obvious bumps. He finished with a notch in the flat end. "Now, give it a try."

I huffed out a sigh, but took the mangled arrow anyway. I notched it into the bow, pulling it back and aiming for the rough target we'd drawn on a convenient apple tree. *Piece of junk*, I thought as I let fly. *This'll never work.*

A second later I dropped the bow in shock, staring at the poor apple tree. The oak arrow had hit the target dead centre…and stuck. "How on earth did that work?!"

"Harmony oak," Kajus said smugly. "I told you, arrows made from its wood do what the maker wants. There's a reason it's banned from competitions."

"Yes, but I was convinced it would fail," I argued. "I wasn't even thinking that I wanted it to work!"

"But I was."

I paused, studying him in confusion. "But...I was holding the arrow."

"But I was the maker," he retorted, smiling. "I was the one to cut the wood from the tree, so it was my intentions that stuck. And I wanted a bulls-eye."

I shook my head as the statement began to make sense. "It might look like Enorian oak," I said finally, "but it really, really isn't. The *maker's* intentions, not the bearer's? That feels dangerous." What if someone gave a hunter an arrow intended to commit murder, so that it struck a friend instead of a deer? How would you ever prove such a thing?

Kajus strode towards the tree and tugged at the makeshift arrow. It was stuck fast, and finally he broke it off rather than removing it entirely. "As I said, Claire. They're banned from competition. But it looks like you won't be impressing anyone with your archery skills, so maybe you should try something else. A hammer throw?"

I looked at him in surprise since 'hammers' weighed about half what I did and were notoriously hard to aim, then realising he was joking, grinned. "And see how many bystanders I can take out accidently? It'll be worse than the archery. You must really dislike your own people."

He took it the way it had been intended, grinning back at me. In spite of his otherwise inhuman appearance, he did have good teeth – straight and white if you ignored the sharpened canines. "We'll just get all the Enorians to sit behind the targets."

"Sure, *that's* the way to create lasting peace."

We laughed, and impulsively I reached out and patted him on the cheek. His fur felt rough, rather like a shaggy dog's, but I found I didn't mind. "Thanks for trying, anyway. I had fun."

Kajus reached his hand unconsciously up to where I'd

touched him, smiling a little hesitantly. "I'm glad you had fun. Maybe we can aim to have you in next year's competition. I could make you a bow – a smaller one, if you like."

Had I been inappropriate, touching him like that? I'd meant to be friendly. I covered up for my possible misstep by joking, "A child-sized one, since the bows seem to be made for giants."

"Haven't we already agreed you're just miniature?" he said lightly. "I can even paint it purple. Then everyone will know it's yours."

I looked at him in surprise. "Why purple?"

He shrugged a little awkwardly. "Every time you have dinner you choose a bowl with purple trim. There's all sorts to choose from, so I was just assuming…"

It was a good assumption. "Purple's my favourite colour, but I hardly ever get the chance to use it. We haven't had any purple dyes available since we left Enoria." I smiled at him, feeling for the first time since I'd come here that I had a true friend. That he'd noticed such a small detail meant a lot to me. "So you can make me a purple bow, and I'll make you…a blue hat?"

"No hats, blue or otherwise. You can make me a scarf, if you like. It doesn't have to be blue."

"I'll see what I can find," I said cheerfully. "Maybe a nice yellow like the roses you get around here." I turned, trying to spot the nearest rose bush, but caught my foot on something instead and went tumbling sideways. "Eek!"

But I didn't hit the ground. Instead Kajus had caught me easily, reaching one hand under my back, so fast I hadn't seen him move. "Careful," he said gruffly, setting me upright again. "There are tree roots hidden in the grass."

So I'd noticed. "Wow, you're really strong," I said, genuinely impressed. He'd caught me with one hand…just one. "And fast, too. Is that a gifted thing?"

He glanced away, picking up his longbow and fussing with the strings. "Some of us are much stronger in half-shift, like I am now. But I think I might have been fast anyway, and you don't weigh much."

"Was that why you changed to half-shift?" I asked curiously. "Because you needed to be strong for something?" He would have just been a boy at the time if he was nineteen now. I tried to imagine him as he would have been; a smaller, darker version of Kanut, wanting to help the men with some difficult building project.

Kajus huffed out a laugh. "Strong? No, Claire, I was showing off for my friends. Most of the time there's no point in being in our other form, not unless we need to scout in the forest or maybe fly overhead. I was just trying to impress everyone with how I could take not just one but two forms, and then that was it." He shrugged, but his humour was gone. "I was stuck like this."

"Oh." I amended my mental image of the young Kajus to a playful boy, strutting about with his friends and performing a party-trick that went horribly wrong. But he'd answered my question about the 'purpose' of the gift, even though when I'd first arrived, Cass had been offended when I'd said the same thing. "We have this saying in Enoria, for when children make silly faces. 'If the wind changes, you'll stay like that.' It's not a curse or anything," I said hastily. "Just a joke."

He was silent for a few moments, and I wondered if I offended him. But then his lips curled in a smile. "I guess the wind changed, hmm?"

"I guess it did," I agreed, smiling in return. Now we just needed it to change back again.

That evening marked a change in our relationship – the beginning of an actual friendship. It was amazing how much more I learned about the Veest from Kajus as opposed to my casual talks with Cass or Sala, like the fact that only tanists wore blue. While Kajus had explained tanistry to me earlier, I still found the concept a bit strange. But it did seem a good idea.

Unlike this self-ruled city within the wild lands of

Nordante, my home kingdom of Enoria was ruled over by just one king, whose son would take his place when he died. That was part of why we left in the first place, because neither the king nor his heir were wise nor careful in their positions. The cities were busy and poor and dangerous, and the king's guards and officials were corrupt. Add the drought on top of that, and we'd been happy to go.

But here in Veestlun, Kanut could watch how the different tanists behaved; the decisions they made; how they treated people. Then he could decide who would be best for the job, and I couldn't help thinking that such an approach was best for everyone.

Kajus didn't seem to mind. As Kanut's son, he automatically became a tanist, but he admitted to me that he didn't really care for leadership. He'd be happy enough to be treated with respect and to do the things he enjoyed.

I could understand that. I didn't want to rule, or even to be a ruler's wife, although I supposed I would just deal with it if it happened. I just wanted to feel valued, and like Kajus, to feel free to do the things that I enjoyed. Oh, and another thing – I wanted to know that the world was better off for me having lived in it, even if it was only in small ways. I thought that we didn't all need to perform miracles or live exceptionally sacrificial lives to make a difference. We just needed to be good to the people around us, and not be afraid to rock the boat when something was important.

Maybe Kajus was my important thing, I mused a few days later. To my disappointment there'd been no more signs of change, not even in his sleep, but I hadn't let myself give up on what I'd seen. If he could change even briefly, even when unconscious, then he wasn't truly stuck. If he could be freed before my people came to visit next week, that would solve a whole lot of problems. I was quite nervous about who would come, how they'd react to the Veest…and how they'd react to the apparent insult of one of their people being betrothed to the only Veest who *couldn't* change back.

One afternoon I was in the laundry room ironing clothing

when Sala came in, and my jaw dropped. Her usually frizzy light brown hair was falling in glossy waves around her face, and it looked beautiful. "What did you do?" I asked in awe. And where could I get some of that?

She patted it a little self-consciously, blushing with pleasure. "It's good, isn't it? A couple of Wyse folk peddling the usual tricks, but this one actually works. It's supposed to last for as long as I keep wearing this necklace, or up to five years." She lifted a long cord out of her neckline, displaying a small, simple pendant. "Handy, right?"

My attention had left her hair the moment she'd spoken that word. "Did you say Wyse? I didn't know they travelled through here."

She nodded, still patting her hair. "We get them every six months or so, coming through and selling love potions, success in business, all sorts. I don't know if the others work, but this was a new one. A new Wyse, I mean-"

"Are they still here?" I cut in.

"They just left an hour ago to head south, through the main road." As I dropped the iron and ran for the door, she called after me, "What about the ironing?"

"I'll be back!"

I got a few strange looks as I raced through the main courtyard, out through the city streets and right for the gates. The single guard held out his spear to stop me going through, and I screeched to a halt, narrowly avoiding getting skewered. "Did some Wyse folk just go through here?" I burst out. "I need to see them, right now!"

The guard blinked at me, then shrugged, pulling back the spear. "You don't come back, it's on your head," he hollered after me. It seemed that even the guards knew my situation, and I'd never spoken to that man in my life.

5
The Wyse

I hitched up my skirts and sprinted along the south road until I was gasping, then slowed to a quick trot. But even that was too much for me, and after what felt like an eternity but was probably only fifteen minutes, I had to stop, leaning against a tree as I panted for breath.

They'd left an hour ago. A whole hour, and unless they moved a lot slower than I did, I was going to really struggle to catch up – if I even could. And what did a Wyse look like, anyway? I'd heard they were winged, but that they could also change their appearance as it suited them. If that was true then I wouldn't know them even if I did catch up. "I'm never going to find them," I moaned desolately.

"Who are you looking for, dear?"

The bright voice came from what was apparently a talking patch of sun-dappled scrub. I did a double-take, then realised it was just a tramp, a plain and plump grey-haired woman, sitting with her large bundle of worldly goods stacked beside her. She wore the same green-brown as our surroundings, and she'd been sitting quietly enough that I'd not seen her at all.

Feeling only a little embarrassed, I quickly explained. "Some Wyse folk came through Veestlun and I really need to talk to them, but I didn't know they were there, so I missed them. I'm trying to catch them now. You wouldn't have seen someone coming through this part of the woods, would you?"

The woman took a sip from her little wooden cup, shrugging. "Depends. What do you want them for? A love philtre?"

That hadn't even crossed my mind, and the thought made me feel odd. What would I do with such a thing, try to make Kajus fall in love with me so he'd change? No, not for an instant, and I wouldn't have done it with Alec either. They'd have to choose me, not be made to choose me. I shook my head. "I have a...friend who's cursed. Sort of. I thought the Wyse might be able to help me."

"And what can you give to someone who'd break a curse for you?"

I was about to say it was none of her business when another person walked out of the woods behind her, coming up and taking another little wooden cup. It was a young man, almost pretty enough to be a girl, and he looked at me curiously before sitting with his companion. And I didn't know how I could explain the feeling I had next, except to say that I felt like whatever I was seeing right then, it wasn't the whole picture – like there was more in front of me than my eyes could take in. No wings, but it didn't mean there weren't any there. Perhaps I'd found my Wyse folk after all.

I opened my mouth, closed it, and thought again. What *did* I have? "I have a silver mirror and a matching comb back in Veestlun," I told them. "But they're part of my dowry."

"Personal belongings only," the woman replied. "What do *you* have?"

A plain brown dress or three? Some old, worn shoes? A pair of oft-mended stockings? Nothing they'd want. And anything really nice I owned wasn't really mine after all. So after a long, crestfallen moment I finally replied, "Nothing that wasn't given to me."

"Remember that," she said, patting the ground beside her. "Come on, sit down with us. Tell us about your beast."

So they knew who I was, and who I was betrothed to.

I sat, but I was offended on his behalf. "Kajus isn't a beast. He's intelligent and kind, and he just happens to be trapped in a half-shifted form."

"Uh huh. And you call this cursed, do you? I believe his kind call him gifted. He looks as the Veest are supposed to look."

Frustrated, I replied, "Only some of the time! And he *feels* cursed, even if he isn't really. He's shut out of so many things, and people react so badly when they see him. How do you expect a girl to-" But I couldn't finish my sentence.

"To love him?" the woman queried. "To truly be married to him, I expect. It's all very well to love someone – and I'm not saying that you do – but you shouldn't marry them when the sight of them makes you gag. Can you, Gaelen?"

The young man shook his head in agreement.

"So the question is, what can we do when the problem isn't a true curse, but an inability to change?" The woman shuffled around inside her bag, then pulled out a small glass bottle with a cork stopper. "This will work like oil in stuck cogs, so to speak, but it only works if the ability is already there. Is it?"

"Yes!" I took the bottle, staring at it in wonder. I could see cloudy liquid swirling around as I moved it, but it didn't look any more powerful than the dregs from a mug of ale. "Not a pendant?"

"You'd be referring to the young lady with the unruly mop of hair," she said with a smile. "No, pendants like that are intended to create an unnatural change. Her hair is naturally curly, but with a little supernatural touch, it'll be silky smooth. But to simply make someone what they ought to be, the change must come from the inside."

"OK," I said thoughtfully. "So he needs to drink it, then."

"Indeed he does," the Wyse woman agreed. "Unless he truly is cursed, in which case the problem will need to be fixed by some other means."

"He's not really cursed," I said again, still studying the bottle. "He's just stuck."

There was a slight pause. "Very well," the woman said. "But even with that remedy, the change may take some time, so don't lose heart. Now in regards to payment…"

I tensed. I'd heard stories about wicked power-users asking for great prices, and I didn't know what kind of person this was. "Yes…"

"We'll call it a kindness offering," she replied briskly. "All I require is your promise that you won't misuse this."

I stammered out agreement, looking back down at the little bottle. Could it really be free? Could it really *work*? "Thank-" I began, but when I looked up again, they'd disappeared, right down to the last bundle of what-evers. And they'd really gone, not just disappeared. I knew because I felt around to see if they were hiding (and if they had been, that would have been awkward). I hadn't even got her name.

But what could the Wyse woman have meant when she'd said I mustn't misuse it? It wasn't like I was going to drink it myself, or sneakily put it into someone's drink…

Oh. I stopped mid-step as I realised what it could have meant. What if Kajus wouldn't agree to drink it? Would I try to trick him into it? It was tempting to think so, but I couldn't imagine that he wouldn't agree. Who wouldn't take the chance to change if they could help it?

"No," he said flatly. "I'm not going to take some unknown substance and get turned into a duck or something. It's not worth the risk."

Now I hadn't expected that response, and I had to work to keep my voice even as we were sitting in our customary dinner spot, surrounded by other people. "But Sala used their product on her hair and it was flawless," I countered, trying not to whine. "What if it does work, Kajus? The Wyse woman said it would just help smooth things along with shifting, not force you into an unnatural shift. You could just-"

"All peddlers will promise all sorts of things," he interrupted. "You think I haven't tried this many times before? After the fourth false promise I just gave up. All those people want is money."

I was quiet only a moment. "I didn't pay anything."

"What? That's even worse-"

"She said it was free!" I cut in. "She said it was a kindness offering, and that I only had to promise not to misuse it. That was all. So even if you're being stubborn and-" pig-headed, I almost said, but held myself back at the last moment, "...and fearful, I'm not going to sneak it into your goblet."

Kajus looked taken back. "You thought about sneaking it into my drink?"

"Thought, not did. I wouldn't have warned you if I was actually going to do it."

He looked down at his half empty goblet, frowning, then back at me. "A Wyse woman actually gave you something for free. Can I see it?" I handed over the little bottle, and he held it to the light, his eyes narrowed. "Did she say how it worked?"

I shook my head. "She said that because you're not cursed, just stuck in half-shift, the best she can do is try to help you shift naturally."

He studied the bottle dubiously, then slipped it into his pocket. "I'll think about it."

Now that could have meant anything, but that evening when we were preparing for bed – him still in his usual place on the fur rug – he said suddenly, "I'll try it, if you like. Just this once. But when it doesn't work-"

"You can say you told me so," I finished, then came around to sit on the side of the bed, watching him. "Go on, then." Inside I was bubbling with excitement. This had to work – I *knew* this would work...

Kajus took the stopper out of the bottle, sniffed at it cautiously, then made a face. "It smells like liquorice. I hate liquorice."

"Then it'll probably taste like cherries," I offered. "Go on."

He shrugged, then lifted the bottle, swigging the whole contents. A moment later he screwed up his nose. "Nope, definitely liquorice. What happens now?"

"You try to change, I suppose. What do the other Veest do when they change?"

"They tell me they just think about changing, and then it works." He put the bottle down carefully, taking a deep breath. "Think about changing…"

One moment he was just standing there on the rug in his furry, pig-faced self, still wearing that day's tanist-blue clothing, and the next there was an actual boar there on that rug, enormous and black and potbellied, straining the same clothing. Its blue eyes widened, and it made a squeal of shock.

"Um," I said, trying not to laugh with shock, "it worked! Now can you change back to human?"

The pig shook its head like shaking off a fly, then suddenly it morphed again and it was a huge black wolf, then another tremble and Kajus was back there as I knew him, on his hands and knees and with clothing worse for wear. He was as beastly as ever, and there was a long moment where we both just sat there, trying to take in what had happened.

"Can you try changing to human?" I asked finally.

He scrunched his eyes shut, waited a bit longer, then opened them and shook his head. "This *is* my attempt to change to human."

"Oh." I was incredibly disappointed, especially as he *had* actually changed, just in the wrong way, but I tried to put a good face on the situation. "Well, at least you aren't trapped as a duck."

Kajus sat up, nervously swiping a hand through his shaggy fur. "I could have been stuck as those other things, and that would have been a hundred times worse than what I am now. I'm *not* doing that again."

I wanted to ask him to try again some other time, but I'd seen the fear in his eyes when he'd been in the other forms, and I wouldn't push. It'd happen with time, right? And if I'd thought it was hard being betrothed-married to someone like him, imagine if he'd been a boar or a wolf permanently…

"Thank you for trying," I said instead. "I appreciate the effort it took, but the Wyse folk did say it could take a while to work."

He shook his head, looking resigned. "I think it's time to just accept that this is who I am. If you can't handle that, then maybe we do need to end this marriage before your human celebrations."

Now this had taken a nasty turn, I realised in dismay. "I didn't say I wanted to end the marriage," I said in a low voice.

"Well, you're not going to marry me properly when I'm like this, are you?" Kajus got awkwardly to his feet. "Now if you'll excuse me, I need some space."

He left, and I couldn't sleep after that. I couldn't argue with what he'd said – I did *not* want to marry him as he was, not in a hundred years, not if I was blind and deaf and lonely…alright, maybe then because I wouldn't know what to expect, but not now. No way.

But I didn't want to end the marriage, such as it was. Yes, it was about the peace treaty between our people, but it was also about our friendship, and about that boy I'd seen so briefly the week before. If I refused to complete the marriage it would be like giving up on the idea that things could ever be different, that he could change.

And let's be clear about this. The problem was on the outside, not the inside. Problems on the inside could be far, far harder to change, and if he'd been an abusive drunk or a philanderer then I'd not have waited for any change. I would have left, since my life was worth more than putting up with that kind of thing. But the half-shift…

As the days passed I didn't mention it again, and I didn't notice any other changes. Kajus didn't say anything to anyone else that I was aware of, and the date of my people's visit came up rapidly. There was a general sense of excitement and nervousness that I felt too – the Veest didn't usually have outsiders in their tournaments. Would they compete well? My people, they meant. They all seemed confident that they'd do well, because they were the awesome Veest, but if my people shot the way I did…it went without saying that we'd lose horribly. And then there were the wedding celebrations planned for the final day of the tournament. I'd be forced to make a final decision on that day, and I couldn't bear to think about it.

The day of arrival dawned, and we watched from above the city gates as my people came up the road: twelve of them plus one wagon-and-donkey loaded with provisions. The Enorians wore those simple clothes that I'd almost come to miss, and I could see their familiar dark hair and skin even from this distance. I'll admit it, I had to hold myself back from bursting into tears and running out to meet them, since that would give the wrong impression of how my time here had been.

As they came closer I began to recognise faces. Walking in the front were the two Streeths along with their son and his wife, my father and my sisters – heaven knew what had dragged Tabitha all this way after her protests, perhaps she did love me after all – and various others who I knew by name but not personally. They were the leaders, the ones who excelled in diplomacy as well as in other areas (barring my sisters, obviously) and the ones who would hopefully keep the treaty intact rather than cause offense and ruin the whole thing. And there, near the back, was Alec.

My heart made a painful *twang* in my chest, and my smile became fixed. Why Alec? Why did life have to rub in my face what I'd wanted and now would never have? But even as I thought that, I remembered Kajus's human form. Perhaps I was just foolish enough when it came to males to always want what I couldn't have. Even if Kajus could take human form, it wouldn't guarantee me his heart – and that was becoming increasingly important to me.

There was a small group of Veest who'd been chosen to greet the visitors: Kanut, half a dozen of the blue-clad tanists, and at the back Kajus and I standing side by side. I could see his tense posture and slightly too-wide eyes, and wondered if he felt as nervous as I did.

But then I saw the moment my family spotted me. Amadine's face lit up, and she gave me a generous wave from her position near the back. I waved back, feeling a wash of love at seeing my sweet little sister, and then I heard her say excitedly to Tabitha, "There's Claire!"

Tabitha hushed her, but with the outburst my own nerves had calmed. I also heard a hum of amusement from behind me, and the whole atmosphere seemed to lighten.

We stood in place during the formal greeting, and I could see my people's eyes flickering over the Veest group, smiling at me – and then noticing my partner, and their eyes would widen. Father must have warned them, because they all kept their mouths shut and for the most part, their expressions even.

But the moment the formal greeting was past and the Enorians were welcomed in the gate, Amadine broke free from the group and rushed up to me, throwing her arms around me. I hugged her back and yes, there might have been a few tears. "I missed you," she whispered in my ear, then turned and looked at Kajus wide-eyed. "Is that your husband?"

"Not quite," he replied, and her eyes grew wider. "By your people's tradition, we'll be married properly in three days, with the celebration."

He didn't turn to look at me, or comment on our earlier conversation (would the celebration even go ahead?) but still that was all I could think of. I felt my cheeks heat.

But knowing none of that, Amadine just stared at Kajus with round dark eyes in her small round face, and asked the most important question. "Will there be cake?"

"Uh…I suppose we could have cake," he replied. He glanced at me. "Will there be cake, Claire?"

I pulled away from the hug, giving my sister a light tap on the shoulder. "Introductions before asking for cake," I told her, then turned her to face him. "Kajus, meet my youngest sister Amadine. Amadine, my…um, betrothed? My husband Kajus."

She was still staring. "Do you turn into a pig? Because you have a nose like a pig."

He didn't blink, thank heaven. "Sometimes. Do you turn into a chipmunk? Because you have cheeks like a chipmunk."

"No!" she cried, outraged, but then realised he was joking and smiled. "Oh. I think my cheeks might change when I get older. Claire's did."

He looked at me quizzically, and I shrugged. "It's true. I used to have rounder cheeks, believe it or not." I wasn't precisely slender now, but at seventeen this was my less 'puppy fat' version.

But the discussion of my roundness (or not) came to a halt when Tabitha came over. There were more hugs, less tears; and again confirmation that Father had been speaking to her. She was perfectly polite to Kajus, even curtseyed, although I did notice that she carefully didn't look at his face. The same with most of the other Enorians that came to speak to us – faces made dear by familiarity rather than by anything else – and I started to relax. Perhaps this would go well after all.

And then Alec came over.

Kajus had just turned away to speak with someone else, and so it was just me and my old infatuation – a whole six weeks out of date. Alec looked remarkably handsome, his hairless brown skin smooth and so, so appealing compared to coarse black fur. But he was visibly upset.

"Claire, are you alright?" he asked in a low voice, leaning in towards me. "Please don't tell me you're actually married to that- to that-"

I felt a hard hand on my arm, and then Kajus was standing next to me, so very close to Alec. "Veest?" he suggested. "And the celebration will be in three days, thank you for asking. I trust you'll be able to show your support?"

Alec pulled away, his curled lip clearly showing his disgust, and I wanted to slap him. Didn't he know what was riding on this? Regardless of what had come before, I'd made my choice for now, and I knew what I had to do.

So before Alec could say anything else destructive, I put

my hand over my almost-husband's, smiling pleasantly up at him. "We haven't made all the arrangements yet, but be sure that you'll be notified."

Alec looked down at our hands, held together over the fabric of my long-sleeved dress, and his expression hardened then went neutral. "Of course. I would never miss such an important occasion in Claire's life."

"And we would never expect you to," Kajus said politely, but behind that politeness was steel. "Are you a relative?"

Alec let out a bark of laughter. "No, we're definitely not related. I'm Alec Tamson. I've known Claire since we were children."

"And I am Kajus, son of Kanut and tanist to the headship of Veestlun. A pleasure to meet you."

Alec gave him a brisk nod, but then with another glance at that hand on my arm he turned and walked away. There were a few long, awkward moments, and then Kajus pulled his hand off my arm. "You said he wasn't interested in you."

He'd remembered that, had he? "He hadn't been," I replied, still shaken over the exchange. Alec's reaction had been the last thing I'd expected, and I didn't know what to make of it. Should I feel pleased about his jealousy, as if it meant he valued me? Because I didn't feel pleased; I felt annoyed at his tactlessness. "I don't know what that was about."

Kajus studied my face thoughtfully. "And what about you?"

"I'm betrothed to you. Married. Whatever!"

"I know that. I meant would you *like* him to be interested in you?"

I quickly looked around, checking no one could hear us, and then retorted quietly, "Of course not. It's incredibly bad timing. If he was interested, he should have said so two months ago. Not now."

"So you're not in love with him."

Was I? My pointless infatuation had just been a part of my life for long enough that I'd thought it was unshakeable, but I'd never called it love. "No," I said finally. "Are you in love with Cass?"

Kajus paused, his jaw tight. "No, and I've barely spoken to her in weeks. You'd know if you'd really been paying attention. But this isn't about people from our past, even when they're right in front of our faces. It's about *my* face. Even though you backed me in front of Alec, I don't know if you're going to follow through with what you said. Are you going to marry me, Claire? Really and truly and legally – by your people's standards – in three days' time? Because you know that to the Veest, we're already married. You're the one who's holding back."

We were surrounded by people, all moving into the city, and now he wanted to talk about this? "Your timing is terrible too," I hissed. "Can we talk about this tonight?"

"You'll be sharing a room with your sisters, and I don't want to talk about this event as if it's going to happen if it's not really."

"Fine. Fine, I want to marry you, but I can't do it until you've changed," I told him, my quiet voice not disguising the importance of what I was saying. "There, I've said it. But you've no right to accuse me of holding back! You insist on sleeping on the rug, Kajus! Like a dog!"

He leaned in towards me until I felt that coarse fur against my cheek, and murmured, "Do you want me to sleep somewhere else?" I couldn't stop myself jerking away from him, and he let out a short, humourless laugh. "Of course not. I know what you think and how you feel about me, Claire, and I don't blame you. Why would you accept what no Veest is willing to? But I won't accept a sham. It's not fair on either of our peoples – or on us."

"Kajus!" How could I say that I just wanted him to change forms, when he wouldn't even try? When he was convinced it was impossible? And so I supposed that to him, our marriage ever being more than just a 'sham' was also impossible.

He walked away from me like he had so many times before, and I didn't stop him.

6
The Games

I threw myself into welcoming my family and the other Enorian visitors, doing my utmost to act content and to show the Veest in the best possible light. It went both ways – my people had to do the same. But except for sweet Amadine, everyone else seemed to be on edge. The conversation was light and friendly, but to me this peace seemed as fragile as a painted egg. One misstep by one careless person, and it would be broken.

I barely spoke with Kajus, but we smiled and sat next to each other at the lavish dinner set by the Veest, rock-like bread and all. I'd grown accustomed to it, but I wondered how long I'd have to live here before I'd be allowed into the kitchens to make those soft rolls that I really wanted.

I glanced across the tables and saw my father, sitting down from me near the Streeths and Kanut, and seeming carefully focussed on his thick stew. Just then he glanced across the table, his gaze fixing on the tall, formidable Mistress Babic, and I hid a smile, remembering my first day here.

But that reminded me of why I'd arrived in the first place. Father had been captured, held as a hostage until I'd come to take his place. Yes, we had peace – sort of – and my people would be moving into a new, fresh, potential-filled home even now. But the whole treaty had been essentially brought about by extortion, and the 'marriage' it was based on might very well not ever be complete. And then what would happen to us all?

Just then Father glanced over towards me, and this time he met my gaze. He smiled a little, but it was a movement of the mouth only. I knew him well enough to see his eyes were creased with worry. I smiled back, trying to convey my hope that everything was OK, that everything would be OK, but I didn't know if he took it in.

I didn't know if *I* believed it.

After dinner, the tables were pushed to the sides of the Great Hall and the first games were set up. These weren't officially part of the tournament, since the results wouldn't go towards choosing the final winner, but I looked around and saw many excited faces. Several of the Veest were carefully setting up a series of what looked like tall, thin wooden jars at one end of the room, and a couple more were carefully sweeping the wooden floor clean. Even though Kajus had ignored me for hours, I leaned over towards him. "What's this?"

"It's called Roll the Ball," he replied. "Look, Father is explaining."

It seemed the goal of the game was to roll a heavy ball along the floor, then hit as many of the thin wooden jars as possible. The Veest called them 'pins', and when they were hit with force, stars! They went flying in every direction. Then a scorer would call out the number hit, another would mark it on a large chalk board displayed on one wall, and the pins would be rapidly reset.

"Ten players per side," Kanut instructed. "Three rolls per player."

"What does the winning team get?" I heard someone call out. It sounded like Alec.

Kanut paused, then a distinctive, small voice shouted, "Cake!"

Everyone laughed, and he waved a hand in agreement. "Cake it is for the winning team. Now choose your players!"

Several Veest assembled on the floor, seeming organised enough that I'd vouch they'd chosen beforehand. Kajus wasn't among them. But there were only a dozen Enorians here at all, and we were short. Tabitha emphatically refused to play, saying she had no aim (as her sister, I could confirm this) and one of the oldest men bowed out too, claiming that he couldn't see more than ten feet in front of his face, and would be a health hazard. Amadine of course was too young, even though she pouted at being excluded.

"What about Claire?" Tabitha suggested. "She's usually good at boules, and that's similar."

Suddenly everyone was looking at me where I stood amongst the Veest, at the front of the spectators. Otherwise I wouldn't be able to see at all.

"Claire is on our side," someone with a Veest accent said. "She can't play for you lot."

"Not yet she isn't," Missus Streeth shot back. "Not 'til the wedding. For now she's ours. Right, Claire?"

"The wedding was six weeks ago," the unseen Veest countered. "She's married. She's a Veest. Right, little Enorian?"

"Uh…" No? Almost definitely not.

"You just called her Enorian," Alec argued. "And she's not wed by our standards, so she can play. Can't you, Claire?"

The light atmosphere had suddenly turned tense, and my head was ringing from the pressure. "Enough!" I exclaimed. To the Veest I said, "I'd be happy to play for either team, but I notice that you locals aren't short a player, and the visitors are. Also, Kajus isn't playing. If he can't play a game like this in his own home, then why should I be allowed to?"

There was a long silence, then Kajus stepped out of the crowd; a standing beast even amongst a strange and beastly people. "I am playing," he said mildly. "I was just popping out for a minute. So you can play for the other team, Claire. It won't be much of a threat if you throw like you shoot."

I smiled at him in relief at the decision being made for me, and that he wasn't excluded from this too. "We'll see, shall we? Do we get a practice throw?"

"Nope," the first of the Veest team said. He was a solid middle-aged man clad in tanist's blue, and he eyed the wooden pins with an almost frightening zeal. "Let's go."

So off we went. First the tanist threw, neatly knocking out eight of the nine pins amid cheers from the locals. Then Master Streeth went with a wide shot, almost knocking out a few of the closest spectators to gasps of horror – although luckily no one was hit. He shrugged, a little ruddy-cheeked, then handed the ball back to the scorer. "The thing's heavier than I expected."

As the game progressed, the noise levels in the room rose with every successful – or not so successful – attempt. I made a point of cheering for both sides, but the competition was intense enough that I wondered if we'd come away with more enmity than we'd started with.

Missus Streeth showed herself to be an excellent shot, hitting all nine pins on her first try, then proved it had been skill rather than luck by doing it again the second time and third time. That was handy, since when my last turn came around, we were substantially behind. Alec had been a decent shot, as had a couple of the other Enorian men. But the Veest knew what they were doing, and it showed. Even Kajus made a good showing, although in my opinion he was disadvantaged by those rough paw-hands.

But Master Streeth had been right: the ball *was* heavy, and it hadn't done my first two shots any good.

"This feels like solid marble," I said, once again almost dropping the thing onto my foot. "Do you have a lighter one for my last try?"

Kanut laughed from his position nearby, even though I hadn't been joking. "What would be the point of that?" He patted me on the shoulder, his big hand with almost as much weight as the ball. "Go on, little missy. Let's see what you've got."

"Go Claire!" Amadine shouted. "We need that cake!"

Everyone laughed again, and I staggered up to the chalk-marked starting line. The pins looked very small and distant when it was me who had to knock them down. But I tried to emulate the better throwers, swinging both arms back and then releasing the ball on the upswing. It flew into the air to land with a heavy *clunk,* then slowly…oh so slowly…began rolling towards the pins. It was slower even than my first two shots, and those ones had gone wide, barely clipping one or two from the side.

I held my breath as it seemed to come almost to a halt right before hitting the pins. But then *tap*…it hit the pin right in the middle, which slowly tipped over….and then hit another pin, which hit several others. It was the slowest roll for the whole game, but within several achingly slow seconds, every last pin had fallen.

There was a startled moment as I took that in. Had I really knocked them all down, with the world's slowest throw? Yes. Yes, I had. I shot both arms in the air, cheering wildly amid the vocal support of the Enorians. "Yeahhhh!!"

Next to me Kajus was shaking his head. "Claire, that had to be the worst throw I've ever seen. How did you do that?"

"Pure luck," I replied, "and perhaps my sister's desire for cake."

"You know your team still lost," he told me. "By at least two dozen points. But I'm sure we can arrange for Amadine to get what she wants."

"This was a good feast," my youngest sister said sleepily. Her face and hands were smeared with dark, sweet-smelling mush, and she'd begun swaying where she sat on the bed we'd share tonight.

"Hands up," I ordered. "Don't get that stuff on the blankets." Because I'd probably end up washing them. Belatedly I added, "And yes, it was a good feast. Wasn't it kind of the Veest to share the cake?"

"They were probably going to share the cake all along," Tabitha said from somewhere behind me. Her tone was flat. "You can't bake a thing like that in an hour. They must have made it beforehand for dessert."

She was probably right, although I ignored her snappishness. Perhaps she'd argued with Hairy Ned before coming – and he notably wasn't here, thank goodness. "I'm glad you two could come," I said instead, realising again how much I meant it. "I missed you both."

"Missed you too," Amadine murmured. Her eyes were almost shut.

"I suppose I did too," Tabitha said grudgingly. "But what do you expect when you're dragged off so suddenly like that to be kept hostage for our good behaviour? For a while we didn't have you *or* Father."

Her tone suggested this was somehow my fault, and I scowled as I scrubbed Amadine's hands and face with a damp cloth. "I'm the one being kept hostage, Tab. I'm *sorry* if you were inconvenienced!"

"Aha! So you do admit you're a hostage!"

I paused mid-scrub, turning to stare back at her. She stood in her feast finery – by our standards, not Veest – with her hands on her slender hips, and an expression of satisfaction on her face. "When have I ever suggested that I was here voluntarily?" I exclaimed.

"You hardly put up a fight coming here, did you? And the whole time we've been here, you've been on the arm of that- that *beast*, smiling and telling us how kind the Veest are, even though we know the exact opposite! And what's worse, Alec says that you seem *happy*! But you're not, are you?" She paused. "You can't be. If that hairy black thing even tried to kiss me, I swear I'd faint with disgust."

My jaw tightened. I couldn't argue with any of it, but that last comment went too far, and hit too close to home. And more so because I didn't know if our conversation was truly private, I gave her a meaningful look and said, "Watch what you say about him. He's a good guy."

Even if he was being a knobhead at the moment. I wanted more than anything to tell her about his shifted form, how handsome he was when human, but to be honest I had no idea what he really looked like. I'd only seen him for a bare few seconds in the dark, and there was no guarantee that I'd ever see that again. He didn't seem to want to change, not enough to actually try.

"He's not so bad," Amadine piped up sleepily. "Tabby is just upset because Ned was being mean."

Mean, was he? That sounded pretty normal for Ned. What was less normal was it being directed at Tabitha.

"I am not!" Tabitha countered quickly. "And Ned is none of your business, little girl."

Amadine showed great maturity by ignoring that comment – or perhaps she was just too tired to argue. She turned to me. "Kajus looks fluffy, like a dog. Is he fluffy?"

"You need to get into bed," I scolded her. "And no, he's not really fluffy. But he doesn't choose what he looks like. He's actually very nice, and intelligent.""Don't tell me you actually care about him," Tabitha said scornfully. "How can you-"

"Tabitha," I cut in, "I'm glad to have you here, but you need to keep your mouth shut. I don't make horrible comments about your betrothed," – much – "so don't you do it about mine."

"I'm sorry," she said after a few moments, and she truly did sound sorry. "But it feels so terrible to know that my own sister will be marrying such a beastly creature, and will be trapped here for life just because the Veest don't want to share. Why did they have to make it like this? Some of the others are actually handsome, and they set you up with *him*?"

Same question I'd asked, and dismissed, but it kept coming back. "He's Kanut's son," was all I could reply. "It is what it is. It's the price paid to stay in this area. Don't you think it's worth it?"

"Yeah, well, you shouldn't have to pay that price."

I didn't like to think of Kajus as a price rather than as a person, and I didn't even go near our discussion today of how I wouldn't complete the marriage until he changed forms. "Then who will?"

And she didn't have an answer to that.

The next day was the start of the tournament – three days of games and contests from archery and hammer-throwing to various strange games I'd never heard of and which you had to be a shapeshifter to take part. That meant Kajus *could* actually compete after all; just not in their usual archery contest. The Enorians sat those special contests out, watching with wide eyes and pretending not to be fascinated and horrified.

Everyone was in their best garb, and I noticed that my people had pulled out the colour that was usually hidden away. I was wearing one of my Enorian gowns with a dark green skirt and pale corset since I didn't have any Veest garb that fit me. Cassiana was supposed to arrange something suitable, but she hadn't got to it yet.

Speaking of whom, here she was. I hadn't spoken to her in depth these last couple of weeks, had avoided her to be honest, since I didn't know how things were between her and Kajus. But today she was dressed in a pure white gown trimmed with gold accents (quite a brave choice considering the ground wasn't all that clean) and her long gold hair flowed down her back, barely held back with two small jewelled clips. She wore no other jewellery besides the globe necklace, but as always she didn't need anything else.

She came up to me while I watched the men's lacrosse, and we watched together for a while as the two teams of six grappled with hooked sticks, trying to hurl the small ball into the nets at either end of the marked space. It wasn't a gentle game.

I winced as yet another stick made contact with someone's legs, and Cass winced with me. "Seems more like a battle than a game, doesn't it?"

Too close to what I'd been thinking earlier. "Then it can replace any real battles," I replied. "Lucky us."

She looked me up and down, seeming to dismiss me in that one glance. "Lucky you, indeed. We know who'd win if there ever was a real battle."

And that was too close to what had been said at first, and what I really feared. "Are we friends or not?"

"What? Of course we're friends."

"Then can you stop making these veiled threats?" I asked calmly, looking her straight in the face. "I could be living here for the rest of my life, and I'd rather we got on. Wouldn't you?"

"They're not veiled threats," Cass retorted, seeming offended. "Just statements of fact. There's more of us than of you, just like...just like your sister there is the beauty of the family, isn't she? Nothing threatening in that, just an observation."

I looked across to where Tabitha stood near the other young girls, her sleek black hair flowing down her back, almost long enough to rival Cass's. Regardless of her horror over my betrothal, Tabitha had managed to clean up nicely today. She was taller than me and slimmer too, with the same wide eyes set in an oval face. When she wasn't scowling, she was quite lovely in a young, Enorian way.

So yes, it was true that Tabitha was prettier than me, and perhaps Amadine would look more like me than our other sister, but it was just one more thing that made me wonder why I bothered with Cass. Things were hard enough without dealing with these frequent, poorly-disguised insults.

"You might be unhappy with your life," I said finally, "but it's no excuse to try to make me miserable. You can speak to me again when you've got something nice to say." I turned and walked quickly away, leaving the games behind.

Cass was unhappy, Alec was unhappy, I was...mostly unhappy, Kajus was a closed book. If it wasn't for the treaty I'd have said that this was all a waste of time. No matter his protests, I still thought Kajus was sweet on Cass. She was nasty in a careless sort of way, but she was very beautiful, and I wasn't. I was 'cute', or so people said, but not the sort that males fell head over heels in love with. And I'd committed myself to staying here, at least until the wedding/ not wedding was finalised...or until everything fell apart, and the treaty with it.

Happy thoughts indeed.

Feeling much grouchier than before, I made my way to a secluded part of the castle orchard, then sat under an apple tree while I tried to gather my thoughts.

"Claire."

The voice was quiet, but I still jolted in surprise. I knew who that belonged to, but why would he be out here instead of at the games? "Alec?"

"I saw you come this way," he said by way of explanation, his face and exposed arms ruddy from exercise but looking as handsome as ever. "I wanted to talk to you."

"OK." I gestured at the ground in front of me. "Excuse me if I don't get up."

After a moment he sat down across from me, looking into my face intently. "Claire, are you alright?"

That was the question of the day, wasn't it? But I didn't want another discussion like the one with my sisters last night. "Let me take a guess where you're going with this. You hate that I had to leave so suddenly, you think it's an insult that I've been tied to someone who can't even take human form, you want me to remember that I'm a hostage for everyone's good behaviour and definitely shouldn't be happy at all...but you don't have any ideas for how to fix the problem."

Alec blinked. "Actually, I was going to say that I'm here for you. If you're unhappy, we can arrange for you to leave. Forget Rose Valley. It's not fair that it was your life for your father's, or your life for all of our comfort. You don't have to martyr yourself."

My jaw dropped. Had I martyred myself? That sounded very unattractive, and I certainly hadn't meant to. "Oh. That's...thoughtful, I suppose."

There was a silence. "Well?" he prompted. "Do you want

me to talk to your father, and to the Streeths? Because I will. I really care for you, Claire."

Hearing him say those words made something twinge inside my chest, but it was a mere echo of what I would have felt before I'd come to Veestlun. Had I changed? I wondered. Or maybe there'd been so few boys amongst our little refugee group that I'd fixated on Alec from lack of alternatives. Not that he wasn't good-looking and athletic and friendly, and so forth. But maybe I wanted more than those things. I wanted true friendship and common interests. Someone who wanted *me*, not someone with no other options.

"In a brotherly way," Alec added suddenly, his eyes wide. "Definitely brotherly."

I rolled my eyes, only a little offended. In all the years I'd known him, I'd never fooled myself into thinking it could be anything more. "Yes, I *know*, Alec. I was just considering the question." But there could be only one answer. "No."

"No? But Claire, they expect you to *marry* that beast in two days! You're...you're an innocent young girl! Do you even know what that entails?!"

He looked appalled, and in spite of the situation I couldn't help laughing. "I might look younger, but I assure you I'm an adult," I said dryly. "The other women talk a lot. So I don't think there's anything I could face that would shock me."

Now I could see Alec's cheeks reddening even through his golden-brown tan. "Talk about...the men, you mean?"

"Of course. What else is there to talk about?" But the blush was spreading to his ears, and while I was fascinated by what that might mean – was he afraid we'd said something about *him*? – there were more important things to discuss. "But never mind that," I said, changing the subject. "I don't want you to call Kajus a beast, or any more of those horrible names."

"But Claire-"

I held up a finger. "No, Alec. It's not fair on him. I've said it to Tabitha, I'll say it to you. He's a great guy. He's smart, and thoughtful, and funny when he wants to be. He's my friend, and…" I paused, then decided to blurt it all out. "He can change forms…sometimes…and he's really handsome too. I know I was made to come here for Father, but if only Kajus could take human form whenever he wanted, and if he wanted me, then I'd happily marry him. Except I don't know if he does want me. He seems to really like this other girl, Cass." Now my cheeks were warming, and I lowered my gaze, embarrassed. Out of all the people to spill my secrets to, I'd chosen Alec?

There was another long, awkward silence. "Oh. Well… that's not so bad, I suppose. You say he can change forms?"

I nodded. "But no one else knows, Alec, and there are… some problems surrounding that. You need to keep that to yourself. But do you see why I'm not trying to run away? It's not a perfect situation," – at all – "…but it's not hopeless, either. At the very least, I'm not going to humiliate Kajus by ditching him in the middle of a festival. We'll work it out, alright?"

"I guess so. But what about this Cass person?"

I pulled my knees into my chest, suddenly glum. "She's this really beautiful Veest girl. You'd have seen her. She was wearing white today, with long golden hair down her back."

Alec looked blank. "I don't remember seeing any really pretty Veest girls."

I blinked at him. "Seriously, you don't remember? I was talking to her right before you followed me out here."

"Oh, *her*. I suppose she's not bad-looking. Way too pale though, like all Veest. Doesn't hold a candle to, say…Tabitha."

My eyebrows shot up. "*Tabitha*?"

"She's pretty," Alec argued, shrugging a shoulder. But his cheeks were darkening in another blush. "Everyone knows that. It doesn't mean anything that I said that."

"I see." But I was studying him with new interest, and just a little disappointment. Tabitha, was it? She was several years younger than him, but not inappropriately so. "You're interested in taking her away from beastly Ned, are you?" *Please, please take her away from Ned!*

"No! Of course not. Just...I have eyes," he finished lamely. "But we're not talking about me! We're talking about your betrothed or husband or whatever. He, um, likes this pale Veest girl, right? Do you know this for certain?"

I shrugged a shoulder. "Yeah, pretty much. She told me Kajus is sweet on her, and he always blushes when her name is mentioned." Kind of like how Alec had when we'd just discussed Tabitha. *Tabitha*.

"He does? How can you tell through that fur?"

"The trick is in the expression." I sighed, leaning back onto my palms in the damp grass. "Just trust me, there's definitely something there between them. But it's stupid, because I don't think Kajus even likes Cass. She can be quite nasty, and they don't seem to have any common interests."

"Hmm. But if the Veest think she's pretty, then it wouldn't matter about the rest of it," Alec said vaguely, his attention half-focused on a nearby shrub. "Men care more about looks than anything else. At least to start off with."

I felt my shoulders slump. Could that really be true? If so, then I might as well resign myself to a long and solitary life – or else drastically lower my expectations for romance.

Just then I heard the crunch of footsteps on gravel. "Claire!" Sala's voice rang through the garden, and she sounded very close.

I gestured for Alec to stay where he was, then stood and stepped out into view.

"I'm here," I called back, and Sala turned to see me, her eyes brightening.

"There you are. Where did you- Oh." She looked past me, and I realised that Alec had stepped out onto the path after me and was standing closely behind. Obviously he hadn't understood my 'stay here' gesture. "Kajus was asking after you, but I didn't realise you were *busy*."

Oops... I hadn't missed the emphasis on that last word. I took a deliberate step away from Alec. This could look very, very bad, but it wasn't. Now maybe if I'd been *Tabitha*... "Not busy, just talking with an old friend," I said lightly. "Where is Kajus now?"

"In your room, I think," she replied, giving Alec a narrow-eyed look. "You go find him, and I'll just help your *friend* find his way back to the tournament."

"We'll talk later," Alec told me, and I just nodded, then turned and headed for the castle.

My thoughts were buzzing, both from old problems and new. Alec's offer to take me away at the risk of everyone's happiness had been a little unexpected, although perhaps I shouldn't have been surprised. He'd never been happy that I would allow myself to be put into this situation. Martyr myself, he'd said – selflessly dying for some cause or another, and being respectfully remembered. *Ah, that wonderful Claire,* people would sigh. *She suffers for all of us.*

Good grief. No thank you! But was it so wrong that I would want peace for all my people? An actual home? Because except for the whole mess with Kajus being stuck in half-shift and probably wanting beautiful Cass anyway, I'd been quite comfortable here in this well-built town amongst lush surroundings. All I'd needed was to see my family regularly, and I might have even been happy.

I suddenly realised I was frowning hard enough for my face to hurt, and made a conscious effort to relax as I reached our room and turned the door handle. *Yes, subconscious self. Those are quite a few obstacles to overcome.*

The door swung open with a creak, and the couple embracing inside broke apart just long enough to stare at me. "Oh! Excuse me," I began, but then my brain finally caught up with what my eyes had already taken in.

Cassiana, her lips and cheeks pink, and her chin lifted defiantly, was holding hands with a dark-haired Veest boy a few inches taller than herself. His handsome face wore a shocked expression, and his intense blue eyes were now fixed on my face. He also wore tanist's blue.

It seemed at least one of my dilemmas had been solved for me.

7
The Treaty

"Claire," the boy said, with Kajus's voice coming from that handsome face. "I'm…sorry."

My mouth opened, then closed, then I finally managed to get a few words out, a little raspy but calm. But inside I hurt. Oh, how I hurt. "I see you found someone you wanted to change for. Congratulations, Kajus."

"Claire," he said again, and he stretched one hand out towards me. We both watched as the pale skin rippled back into coarsely-furred, claw-tipped paws, and then he pulled back, his expression dismayed. The moment his hand was back by his side, back by *Cass*, it returned to human form.

I sucked in a breath, feeling the back of my throat burn and my eyes prick with unshed tears, then I spun on my heel and left. I couldn't stay any longer, and I couldn't watch Cass's triumph.

Beauty and the beast indeed. My Wyse gift had worked, just not for me.

I went back to the games, and I didn't say a word about what I'd seen, instead trying to focus on what was playing out in front of me. It wasn't easy. All I could think about was Kajus's face, and his hand in Cass's, and how he'd changed back to beastly once he'd reached for me.

He'd reached for *me*, but it was for nothing. We didn't have a chance. *I* didn't have a chance, and the dark, terrible truth played over and over in my head.

But he was much better-looking in the daylight, I did admit to myself. Far more so than the glimpse of moonlit skin had shown me. A match for Cass, not for me. So it looked like I'd be coming back to the Enorian tent-settlement after all, although I figured that without the kind-of marriage to back up our peace treaty, we'd be soon looking for a new place to settle. *Goodbye, Rose Valley.* Unless I could convince Kanut that we would be good neighbours, or that Kajus's change was due to my hard work in getting the potion. I didn't sprint down the road for just anyone.

"Your turn, Claire." I looked down to see a long, metal-tipped wooden dart being pressed into my hand. "Go on."

I lined up the dart with the wooden target propped up ten feet away, but my thoughts were still buzzing. Stupid Kajus. Talking about *me* holding back when he was getting cosy with his old sweetheart! And stupid Alec – I knew he'd never liked me like that, but to be sweet on Tabitha? My annoying, sharp-tongued younger sister? Life was so unfair!

The dart hit the target hard, somewhere around the outer edge.

"One point," the scorer called out. "Eliza, grab that dart, will you?"

To my surprise I realised that 'Eliza' was Missus Streeth, and she'd been sitting here along with a couple of Veest, helping to run the event. But when she got up to remove the dart I'd thrown, she had to brace one hand on the frame to pull it out. "Heavens above, Claire," she exclaimed. "You don't need to throw it so hard! Try throwing it more softly, and your aim might be better."

Stupid handsome Kajus. Stupid triumphant Cassiana, who'd stolen the effects of my own Wyse gift, but didn't even like him. Not really! She just liked that he might rule one day, or so I figured. He'd stay a tanist now. I knew that much.

"Claire!"

My head shot up to meet Missus Streeth's stare, her eyebrows raised. "Everything alright, Claire?"

"Fine," I replied, my tone clipped. *Except that I never get what I want. Oh, and the peace treaty is probably void, but somehow that doesn't feel like the worst thing today.* "Now excuse me, I'm going to have a turn at the hammer throws."

I didn't actually end up throwing one, which was probably a good thing, because Kajus came back out and if I'd got it off the ground, I might have ended up throwing it at him instead. He was minus Cass and back to his usual hairy, hideous self, and I felt miserable seeing him. He hadn't wanted me enough to change for me.

I sat down on a bench in a quiet part of the castle, back from the action, and looked at my feet. I could see him from the corner of my eye, taking a seat next to me, then slumping forward to rest on his elbows.

After about a minute of silence I heard him sigh. "Are you going to keep ignoring me, Claire? I thought you'd be happy for me."

"Happy about what? That you finally got what you wanted? A human form, and Cassiana, and to remain a tanist. I am happy for you. Really."

Kajus made a strange sound in the back of his throat, almost like a growl. "Claire, *you* are my betrothed. I didn't mean-"

"To what? Kiss her?" I kept staring at my feet in their usual brown leather, as if fascinated by an imperfection in a seam. "Let's be honest, Kajus. Neither of us chose each other. I just wanted somewhere for my people to live, and safety for my father. You…" I finally turned to look at him. "What *did* you want?"

He shrugged those bulky shoulders. "Peace. To please my father. It was his idea, you know. But I didn't kiss Cass, Claire. We were just talking, and she took my hand, and then…" He shrugged again helplessly. "I changed, just like that."

I ducked my head again, feeling angry and rejected, and then even angrier because I didn't want to feel that way. Our match had been arranged under terrible circumstances, and I wasn't supposed to care about him. Yet I did. "I guess you finally wanted it enough."

"But that's the thing!" he exploded. "I didn't want it any more than I had any other time since this all happened. Claire, if I could have changed from wanting, I would have done it that night when I drank the potion, with you. But I couldn't! So why now? Why with Cass, and only with her?"

I looked at him again, one eyebrow arched. "Because you're in love with her, idiot. You have been for years." "No, I'm not."

"Yes, you are. Everyone knows it."

"No, I'm not, Enorian! I know how I feel." I opened my mouth to argue, and he raised a hand. "Let me finish. I'll admit there's something there with Cass. Some kind of...bond that I can't shake. Maybe it's just attraction. But the world is full of pretty girls, and it's a whole lot harder to find one who you genuinely like to spend time with, and who seems to like you back. But that's not Cass. I thought...I thought that in spite of everything, it was you."

My head shot up again, and my heart did a double-beat in my chest. Some of the pain receded, but not entirely. He was saying he would choose me over Cass – but that was no longer even a choice. I knew what I had to say. "I do like you," I managed to say. "I thought I'd been clear about that. But you must also know that we never...I'd never want to be more than just your friend, unless you could take human form. With *me*."

There was a silence, and Kajus hung his head. "I know."

I sighed heavily. "So what do we do now? We'll have to tell everyone what's happened, but I don't want the treaty to be ruined. We need peace, Kajus. And the Enorians need somewhere to live."

"I know," he said again. "You know how you said that it seemed my people were trying to get you to break the marriage, thinking then your people could be driven away?"

"Yes?" I'd mostly dropped that idea, even though I still felt like some Veest were unfriendly.

"You were right."

"What!?"

"Shush!" Kajus leaned in towards me a little, his voice lowering. "That's what Cass came to tell me today. I'd been wanting to talk to you about the celebrations planned for two days' time, and Sala went off to find you. But then Cass showed up. She said that someone is plotting to ruin the tournament and trying to get you to leave, so that there'll be an excuse for war. We mustn't let that happen."

"Of course we mustn't!" I hissed. "Who was it? Have you told your father?"

He shook his head. "Cass took off after you showed up, then I came straight out to find you. Except...Sala said you were talking with your, um, Arric. And then you were mad at me."

Quick work, Sala. Thanks a lot. "He's not my Alec," I said, but my thoughts were far away. "He likes my sister. But Kajus, this is important! We need to find out who it is, or this could be really, really bad!"

"He likes your sister? Which one?"

"Not the ten-year-old," I snapped, rolling my eyes. "Come on, Kajus! Imminent war, right?"

"Not imminent," he countered. "We'll just have to be careful. But this Ar- *Alec* definitely isn't courting you?"

I finally calmed down enough to stare at him in disbelief. "He thinks you and I are betrothed or married or whatever, so no. But even if we weren't...*aren't*," I stressed, "he still wouldn't be courting me. He sees me like a little sister. But is this really important, Kajus?"

"It is to me," he muttered. Then those sky-blue eyes flicked to my face. "We'll go talk to my father, shall we?"

And in spite of the circumstances, I was left thinking about how he'd cared so much whether Alec was courting me...or not.

We found Kanut on a balcony overlooking the orchard, just near where the final archery competition would shortly be held. He sat around a food-laden table along with a couple of blue-clad tanists, the Streeths, and my father, who had Amadine in his lap. They all had the reddened cheeks and good cheer that indicated a drink or two had already been had. Except for my sister, of course, whose attention was focused on what looked like toffee on a stick.

"Son, little Claire!" Kanut cheered. "We've just been planning your wedding celebration, Enorian style. The little one tells me there's to be a dress, and presents, and cake. Should be an excellent time for all!"

Good timing. I sucked in a nervous breath, and my hand tightened where I held Kajus's arm. With his thin coat over that thick fur, it felt rather like he wore a fluffy jacket. If only it could be taken off so easily.

Everyone watched us expectantly while I waited for Kajus to answer, but he just stood in silence, and something occurred to me. He really did want his father's approval, to the point where he'd agreed to wed a complete stranger, and even now perhaps feared to give bad news. That was something else we had in common.

So I found myself blurting out, "We have good news. Kajus can change forms!"

That drew a flurry of exclamations from the Veest, who completely understood what it meant, and Kanut's eyebrows shot up almost to his forehead. "Change forms?"

"Yes, to human," I added. "He took a Wyse remedy a while ago, but it just happened today."

A flurry of emotions rushed over Kanut's face, from hope to disbelief to excitement. "Go on, lad," he urged. "Show us! I haven't seen your real face in...er..."

"Almost five years," one of the tanists said. She was fair-haired and middle-aged, and eyed us with perhaps a little less friendliness than the others. I vaguely recalled her harshness in the meeting room when I'd first arrived. Yet here she was with the others – the 'inner circle'.

"Almost five years," Kanut agreed eagerly. "Go on."

"That's the thing," Kajus replied, finally able to speak. "I can't do it all the time. Only when I'm with, um…"

"Claire?" Amadine piped up.

"Er…no. With Cassiana."

"My Cassiana?" the fair-haired tanist asked in shock.

"Yes, Missus Daphne," Kajus confirmed. "Your daughter."

There was a long silence, and I felt my cheeks burn as everyone seemed to stare at the two of us – or more importantly, my hand on his arm. I let my hand drop.

"Right," Kanut said finally. "Someone go get the girl, and we'll see for ourselves."

Twenty minutes later, Cass had been retrieved from some back room of the castle, and was surrounded by a crowd of excited spectators. Her pretty face was wide-eyed, but then her chin lifted high as dozens of hands pushed her towards Kajus. I couldn't help thinking that for such a proud, confident girl, she was acting unusually uncomfortable at being the centre of attention.

Man stealer.

But then from what she'd told me, *I'd* been the one to steal Kajus from her, hadn't I? Or not, if you asked him. I didn't know what to think, or where poor, expendable Damon fit into things.

"Well, go on. Take his hand," someone with a Veest accent shouted.

Kajus cautiously reached out his hand to her and she finally took it, then the crowd sighed in unison as the change came over my former betrothed. Within moments the beastly pig-wolf was gone, and there was human Kajus, his expression of pleasure and confusion so much clearer on

91

this new face. He stood there opposite his father, looking like a much younger, smooth-skinned version of Kanut, whose own face began to screw up as if suppressing emotion.

Then a woman started crying, and the two were surrounded by well-wishers. I slipped back out of the crowd to stand with my family and the other Enorians.

"Well, that's an improvement on his looks," Missus Streeth remarked finally.

"He's still too pale," Tabitha commented. She'd shown up along with everyone else, drawn by the excitement. "But better, I suppose, even though he's not especially handsome. But what luck! The betrothal's broken and you didn't even have to do it, Claire!"

"What do you mean?" Amadine asked. She sounded displeased. "What about the wedding party?"

"She can't marry him when he's with *her*," Tabitha pointed out.

Everyone turned to stare at the couple in the centre of the chaos; both tall and pale-skinned, but such a contrast in their hair colours. Two good-looking Veest (or not, if you asked Tabitha) holding hands. Was it my imagination that made their expressions seem so strained?

"I think she still can," Amadine argued. "I like Kajus when he's fluffy."

"Then you'd be the only one," Tabitha retorted.

I didn't comment, just watched them. Then I felt a warm arm wrap around my shoulders.

"The problem I see now," my father said thoughtfully, "is what happens with the treaty." He looked down at me. "You'll be coming home with us, love. The question is whether we still have a home to go to."

"Of course you do," Kanut said stoutly later that night. We sat in the round-table room, as I thought of it, with all ten of the tanists including Kajus, the half-dozen oldest Enorians, and I. Kajus had returned to his usual beast form, Cass having escaped after having spent the whole afternoon practically tied to his side. "We're not going to push you out of Rose Valley just because things didn't work out with little Claire and my boy. We've had a good time, haven't we? Who knows what could happen next?"

"Hold on, Kanut," Cass's mother interrupted. "You're in a good mood because your boy finally shifted back, and just in time to keep his position and wed someone of real worth. But that doesn't mean we're going to give up that rich valley, and for what? What has really changed to mean we must give up anything to these...*foreigners*?"

That last word was said with disdain, as if she'd wanted to say something different, and I heard the sucked-in breaths that meant imminent arguments from multiple sources. I couldn't blame them, since she'd insulted the Enorians and me all in one go. And Cass, being of 'real worth'? Only to her mother.

"What a cow," someone muttered from beside me. It sounded like Master Streeth, who'd had more than a few honey-sweetened ales throughout the day, and they'd loosened his tongue.

"I am not a cow," Daphne snapped back. "I am a Veest, and my other form is a majestic eagle!"

I caught sight of Kajus's expression across the room; the set of his eyes showing he shared my opinion – amused disbelief – and I almost laughed even though it *really* wasn't the time for it.

"He's saying you're being nasty for no reason," Missus Streeth shot back. "And you are. What's it to you, woman? Your people aren't using the valley!"

"It isn't nasty to protect one's own interests!"

"From who? Cake-loving ten-year-olds?" Missus Streeth swept a hand towards me. "Well-mannered cuties like this one here? Oldies like us who can't even bowl straight? What are you protecting yourself from?"

Kanut raised a hand to speak, but I suddenly found myself standing, and the attention of the whole room was on me. Startled, I coughed. Then when no one shouted me down, I said, "I have something to say."

"Go on, Claire," Kanut said generously. He shot a glare at Cass's mother. "And everyone will keep their mouths shut long enough to listen. We only *look* like animals sometimes."

Stars above, what *was* I going to say? My pent-up frustration and confusion had given me the urge to stand, but I certainly hadn't thought it through. So I took a deep breath, prayed for my brain to make connection with my mouth, then spoke. "I agree with both of you."

"Claire!" more than one person scolded.

"Please listen," I continued. I felt so nervous, but also felt the urgency of the situation. We *must* have peace. "I understand what it's like to be scared. I'm the smallest person in this room, and as everyone keeps telling me, I don't look like much. I'm not scary, and I couldn't change into a manticore or a tiger, or even shoot an arrow straight unless it's made of harmony oak. So it was hard for me to come here, and I only did it because I thought there was no other option. Because I was told my father would be held hostage until that happened, and that my people would have to keep moving, looking for a safe place to live.

"So I tried hard not to think of how scared I was, and I started to get to know you all. And Kajus and I became... friends. That wasn't easy for either of us, and I don't want to lose it just because a few people can't or won't get along. I want us all to be friends. Isn't friendship valuable on its own?"

"I hear what you're saying, little girl," Daphne said. "But there can be no true friendship when you give up nothing, and we give up everything. There'll be resentment. Best you move on now."

That started another outburst, this one intense enough that I thought weapons might be pulled. I just stood there, my hands clenched in fists, trying not to show my fear, unsure whether to sit down or not.

But then Kajus shot to his feet. "What is wrong with you all?" he burst out. "I'm the one who looks like a beast, but it seems that you lot don't know the basics of human decency! Veest, we have more than we need! These are people, human beings who share the same language and similar customs, and who we can sit down with for a drink of ale. They've had to leave their homes, and now they have nothing. Not even dye for their clothing! Why are we acting like they're the enemy? Why are we being so greedy? In this moment I'm *ashamed* to be Veest."

There was a stunned silence, and then Master Streeth began clapping loudly. "Couldn't have said it better, boy. Well done."

Daphne gave him a dirty glare, then scowled at Kajus. "Boy, you've forgotten who your loyalties lie with."

"And you've forgotten that you're only one tanist," Kanut snapped, "and that I rule Veestlun. Mind your tongue, Daphne. And let it be known that the first goal for our people is peace, and anyone – anyone at all – found damaging that goal will be counted as a traitor."

There was another silence, and then a different tanist cleared his throat. He was a man in his thirties, mild in appearance and silent up 'til now. "I too want peace," he said. "But you must acknowledge that the Enorians only gain, while we have given up much. What will they give to us, to make this treaty fair? To make it last? Because Daphne is right. Any resentment will fester, no matter how much you'd will it otherwise."

Kanut leaned back in his seat, his brow low and his earlier joviality now completely gone. He huffed out a heavy sigh. "I will consider it. For now, the tournament continues, and our *guests* will be treated with all the hospitality we can muster. Remember, my boy has finally been freed from his curse!"

There was some quiet muttering at that, but the room emptied. I heard Kajus say to his father, "So we're not pretending it was a gift anymore, are we? But you know it's only a partial freedom."

Out of the corner of my eye I saw Kanut cup his son's face in one big hand. "It's enough."

And it was. Enough to keep Kajus a tanist. Enough to break a betrothal/marriage and maybe even a treaty.

Kajus caught up with me as I walked back towards the Great Hall. "That was a good thing you said there."

Had it been? I shrugged. "I just tried to say how I felt. But stars above, Kajus. After all of this, I can't help thinking that both our peoples can be remarkably stupid."

"Stubborn, scared, possessive," he suggested. One corner of his mouth curled under that piggish snout. "The worst parts of people. Maybe if we spend enough time together, we can show them the best too. Humour, kindness, loyalty."

I did really smile at that. "If only. But Kajus..."

"Yes?"

My voice lowered. "I hate to say it, but Daphne's right. Your people give up something, and ours gain it. But for what? How can we make your people truly content to let us live in Rose Valley? For most of them, sheer kindness or generosity won't be enough."

He sighed. "I don't know, but we'll figure it out."

We would? That didn't sound promising, because I had no ideas.

"Oh, and I got something for you." And then something thin and brown was shoved unceremoniously into my hand.

I glanced at it in disbelief. "A stick?"

"Don't be obtuse. It's a harmony wood arrow. I sharpened and polished it, and it should go anywhere you want it to go." Kajus shuffled in place. "Even throw it, if you want. Just not at me."

"Why would I throw it at you?" I asked absently, studying the arrow. It looked rather like the one he'd found for me back in the orchard, only much smoother, and with a sharply-pointed end. "Have you done something?"

"Nothing new. But when you saw me with Cass, you looked...well, like you'd like to throw something at me."

"Oh." I looked up at him, so much taller than me, with the fur on his head adding to that height. "I suppose I did. I thought you'd kissed her, and never mind that our marriage...

betrothal thing was forced, I'd expected better from you."

"Then I'll be grateful that I gave this to you now, rather than this morning like I'd planned." My eyes widened, and he added, "But I was thinking about what you said, about how our marriage was forced on you. On us both, but it would have been worse for you, with the threat to your father. It wasn't right, Claire."

He said it so earnestly that I wondered if it was new to him. "You only just figured this out?"

"Well, no. I mean, I knew the circumstances weren't good, and I thought it was a miracle that you seemed to like me – or were pretending to. But it wasn't until today that I realised how wrong it was. Claire, if I *am* freed from this curse fully and completely…"

"Yes?"

"…then I don't want to marry you. Not like that."

My heart sank, and my hand fell to my side, still holding the arrow. "Oh. That's alright, I suppose. It was forced on you too, and we haven't known each other long."

Kajus shook his head. "No, you don't get it. People have arranged marriages all the time, so I think nothing of that. I meant I don't want you to marry me only because it's your only option, because your people will have to leave otherwise. I really like you, but I don't want that kind of marriage."

"Oh," I said again. I didn't know what to make of that. "So…where are you going with this?"

He shrugged those big, fluffy shoulders, and an expression came over his face. One that was familiar, but I couldn't quite place it. "I mean that I want you all to have a home in Rose Valley. You can live there, and…maybe I could come to visit. Or you could visit us here."

I looked at him, at his black-furred, pig-nosed beastly form, and felt a wash of affection. He was my friend, even if it seemed he could never be more than that. "I'd like that," I replied sincerely.

"I would too." And then Kajus's face showed that odd expression again, and I finally identified it as the same one he'd had with Cassiana. A blush.

Stars above. Maybe he did like me. *Me,* but it seemed like there were a thousand obstacles in our way, and neither of us knew what we wanted. "We should go back to the games," I said finally.

Drama, drama everywhere. But for now, we would pretend to party.

8
The Revelation

Over the next few days the games continued, as did the feasting and the rivalry. It seemed that everyone was trying so hard to maintain the 'peace', and at every meal Cass sat next to Kajus close enough that their arms could brush, and that he maintained that human form. Sometimes I would see him looking at me, and I'd smile tightly then turn back to my conversation with whoever was closest.

As for my people, we smiled and played and drank, but there was the undercurrent of fear. As Tabitha said to me one night, "I'm so glad you're not trapped into that marriage, Claire. But what will happen to us all?"

I didn't know the answer. So I changed the subject and asked, "Are you still going to marry Ned?"

I expected her to act surprised at the question, but instead her expression darkened. "Maybe," she replied, then wouldn't talk to me any longer.

Interesting.

It was with some surprise that I found Cass alone in the ironing room two days later, when she should have been down at lunch in the Great Hall, hanging off Kajus's arm just like all the previous meals. She sat in the corner of the room, her apron held up to her face. Her eyes were red and her face was wet with tears.

"Cass?" I exclaimed in dismay. "What's the matter?"

She jumped, but then upon seeing me, rolled her eyes. "Oh, it's just you. What do you want?"

"Mistress Babic says she sent you to get tablecloths an hour ago. I said I'd come get them instead." It had been hard to break my habit of helping around the castle, especially since I'd done it for six weeks. I didn't like being waited on. "Why are you crying? I thought you wanted Kajus."

Cass sneered. "I said that, didn't I? But I didn't mean it!" She threw her wet apron onto the floor with sudden emotion. "I touch his hand once, *once*, and this happens? Suddenly everyone's expecting us to get married! I don't *want* to marry Kajus, beastly or human!"

My jaw tightened, and I set my hands on my hips. "Now just one moment. This entire time we were together you were making snarky little comments about how he'd been your suitor, how he was sweet on you – you even flat-out said you wished I would leave him, and you implied that he didn't want me enough to change forms. He apparently wants *you* enough, because you were damned well touching him in *my* bedroom! And now you don't want to marry him?!"

My voice had risen to a yell, something which hardly ever happened, but Cass had barely taken the bait. She was sniffling, and had raised her hands to cover her face.

"What do you want, then, blessed girl?" I asked in frustration. "What do you want?"

"I want Damon," she finally whispered.

"What?"

"I've said it once, I'm not going to repeat it," she said, showing a hint of her usual snap. "Damon. I want to marry Damon, and he wants to marry me."

One, two, three moments of silence, then my voice came out surprisingly even. "So you *were* seeing him. Then what on earth was going on with Kajus?" *You selfish, two-faced cow!*

"My mother doesn't approve of Damon, because he's not a tanist," she said in a small voice. "But if Kajus would just have stayed unchanged for the full five years, then Damon would have taken his place. Then we would have married, and whatever happened next wouldn't matter."

I shook my head. I'd known that Damon was related; mild, milk-white pretty Damon, but I'd never considered that he was almost a tanist. What had he said to me, that he was expendable? "I still don't understand how this fits in with you flirting with Kajus. Why would you do that if it was Damon you wanted?"

"Just a little flirting," she said defiantly. "It didn't mean anything. It wasn't supposed to turn out like this, with *me* half-betrothed and having to hold his hand every other moment, and with Damon in exactly the same damned place as always, out of line to rule. We've made things worse, not better!"

Then her face crumpled again, and she began sobbing into her apron once more. "So many years we've waited, Damon and I, with me having to explain to my mother why I won't accept any other suitors, having to pretend to be awful so that no one wanted me, but still paying just enough attention to Kajus to keep the spell-" But then suddenly her eyes widened, and she stopped speaking mid-sentence.

I'd been so caught by her comment about 'pretending' to be awful that I didn't immediately realise what she'd said. Then the words finally made sense in my head. "Did you just say something about a spell?"

Cass just stared at me owl-eyed, and her mouth opened and closed. She didn't speak.

Could it really be? "You said 'paying just enough attention to Kajus to keep the spell'," I repeated, my voice rising again along with my anger. "Keep what spell, Cass? Is there some kind of spell on Kajus keeping him stuck in half-shift? Keeping him trapped so Damon can be a tanist and you can marry him?"

"Of course not," she finally replied with a little of her usual confidence. But her eyes didn't meet mine, and her fingers were twisting anxiously at her neckline where her ever-present pendant hung.

Suddenly my mind flashed back to Sala's pendant, the one she now wore to keep her hair smooth. It had been plain and she'd kept it tucked within her bodice rather than on display like Cass's, but otherwise it looked quite similar. And that Wyse woman had said that such pendants were for changing the natural state of things. Making things *other* than what they ought to be…and she'd asked me twice if Kajus was truly cursed, not just 'stuck'.

I sucked in a deep breath, my eyes fixed on that pendant. Then when I spoke again, my voice was low. "I've never seen you without that necklace, Cassiana. Where did you get it?"

She dropped it immediately, then tucked it inside her dress. "It was a gift. What's it to you?"

"Nothing at all." But that was a lie. A huge, colossal lie, because I was planning to go straight to Kajus with what she'd just said, and what I'd seen. Somehow we'd get to the bottom of this – a dark, murky, unexpectedly deep bottom. "I better bring Missus Babic those tablecloths," I said instead. "She's been waiting." I grabbed an armful of the nearest linen, then quickly turned towards the door…and ran *smack* into someone's chest.

"Ow!" I bounced off and landed hard on my backside on the wooden floor, and the linen scattered.

"Cass?" It was Damon, and his pale face was set in harsh lines I'd never seen him wear before. "And the Enorian. What are you doing in here?"

"I came in to get some tablecloths," we both said at the same time, then she glared at me. I would have laughed, except it wasn't at all a laughing matter.

"Cass was upset over the current turn of events," I said as I picked myself up, and I could hear the bite of unhappiness in my own tone. "You might want to comfort her. I better get going."

It seemed as if it would work. Damon moved as if to go past me into the room, and I was an inch away from slipping out when hard fingers gripped my arm. He'd snagged me almost thoughtlessly, his attention seemingly fixed on the other girl. "Everything OK, Cass?" he asked mildly.

She should have snapped back at him – it seemed in line with her personality up 'til now – but instead her whole posture sagged. "Don't let her leave," she replied in a dull, flat voice. "I said too much, and she's not stupid enough to overlook it."

Stars, then there *was* a spell. Uh oh. I yanked hard at where Damon held me, but all it gained me was friction burn. "Cass exaggerates," I said through gritted teeth, trying to sound casual. "So you two have a romance. Kajus already told me that, and that her mother disapproves. But that doesn't give you leave to manhandle me!"

Damon ignored me, instead pulling me inside the room and shutting the door as easily as I would have managed, say, Amadine mid-tantrum. It was quite disheartening. "What did you say to her?"

He'd been asking Cass, not me. "I spilled about there being a spell, and she figured out about the pendant," Cass replied. She sniffed, swiping a hand over her face. "I'm so sorry, darling, but everything's been weighing on me! Who would have thought it would lose effectiveness so quickly?"

"Five years, Cassiana. Five years of putting my head down and waiting for the timeframe to pass, and you mess it up three months in advance?" Damon threw up his free hand in frustration, but didn't let go of me. "I told you not to touch Kajus. Talk to him I said, flirt with him and keep his attention when you need to, but do *not* touch him."

"I was trying to talk to him. I was, I swear! But he's been ignoring me more and more, and I could feel my influence slipping these past few weeks. And then today, he was going to walk away from me! So I didn't think, I just grabbed his hand-"

"You didn't think. And it seems you couldn't keep your mouth shut either." His voice was still low, but it shook a little with what had to be anger or fear. "It seems like your mother and Kanut would have the two of you betrothed in an instant. What are we supposed to do now?"

103

"I'm sorry," Cass whined. Then her face crumpled again and she slumped back into that chair, her shoulders shaking. "I don't know what to do. We can't give up, but I don't know what to do now."

This whole time I'd been tugging my arm, trying to escape, but Damon had a grip like iron. "Um," I said. "I hate to interrupt your special conversation about something I completely don't understand, but you do realise that Kajus was already shifting, right? Without you touching him, Cass. He did it at night, but we didn't tell anyone. It was only a matter of time before it happened publicly."

Their eyebrows shot up almost comically, and I added, "So the two of you should just grow some ba...*courage* and tell the truth. I don't care what you've been up to," – OK, so that was also a lie – "...but this isn't going to get any better if you just let things happen. Tell Daphne that you're getting married, then just do it! Or even run off and do it first, then come back with a baby or two. They can't argue then."

The two of them blinked at me for long moments, then Damon remarked, "Nice try, Enorian. But we're not letting you go, and we're not running off, either. If we do that, I'll never be a tanist."

"And he *deserves* to be a tanist," Cass added snarkily.

I looked at their solemn faces, and that infuriating grip on my arm, and for the first time realised I could be in real danger. Maybe I could have escaped from one of them, but not both. I gulped. "Are you going to kill me?"

"No!" Damon snapped, just as Cass shouted, "Of course not!"

"But we can't let you go or you'll tell," he added. He huffed out a sigh, then swore under his breath.

"What about the other influencing spell?" she asked quietly. "You kept it as a backup, thinking to use it on Mother if this went wrong. What if we used it on the Enorian?"

Influencing spell?! OK, I was done being well-behaved. I suddenly dropped my weight to the floor, and as I felt Damon stumble over me, I swung my fist hard. I hit him somewhere in the leg – not the most effective place – but was finally free. I scrambled for the door handle, letting out the biggest, loudest scream I could summon as I did so.

But the other two were acting fast, and someone slammed the door shut in front of me. Someone else pulled me away, and cloth was shoved in my mouth. I struggled and elbowed and kicked whoever it was, but it was no good. I felt myself shoved to the ground, my arms twisted behind my back, and the hard wood pressed against my face. Was someone *sitting* on me? I'd never hated being small as much as I did in this moment. What I would have given for a good sharp knife. And I couldn't even reach the harmony oak arrow in my waistband…

You monsters! I tried to shout, but through the gag it was more like, "*Ooo onnffff!*"

"Keep her quiet!" Damon hissed from somewhere above my head. "And get the hair!"

Hair? What hair? Just then there was a sharp bite of pain on my scalp, and I heard Cassiana say, "Oops. Ugh, she's bleeding. Will this do?"

"It'll be fine."

There was a sound like metal scraping, then Damon said, "Claire the Enorian, I hereby place you under my influence, to do as I will, until I choose to free you."

I'd been fighting madly (and fruitlessly) up 'til this point, but suddenly my limbs were heavy. Too heavy to fight, too heavy to move. I felt my face fall slack around the cloth gag.

"Did it work?" I heard Cass ask.

"She's not trying to kick me anymore, so I'll say yes."

Just then a knock sounded at the door. "Everything OK?" I heard a gruff voice call through the heavy wood.

Kajus.

My hopes rose, and I tried to call out, to move that gag from my mouth. But even though I was raging on the inside, outside I was as useless and silent as a carved wooden doll. Above me I heard hurried whispers. Then Damon whispered, very quietly and very close to my ear, "I command you to act normally, and don't tell a word about our secrets. Not in word, not in deed. Not even a hint."

"Hello?" Kajus called again. I heard the door handle rattle. "Is Claire OK? It sounded like she screamed."

Oh bless you and your excellent hearing, Kajus. But I still couldn't move, and Cass called back, "She tripped and hit her head. But she's fine."

No I am not! Because even though the gag was removed, and the weight lifted off my back and I could move to my hands and knees, I couldn't say a word.

There was a pause. "Will you let me in?"

"I don't want to hold your hand right now, Kajus," Cass said sharply.

I stood shakily. The two others were watching me warily, and I could see Damon was holding something in one hand. A pendant? But then he shoved it in his pocket. *Act normal*, he mouthed.

"I'm not here to hold your hand, Cass," Kajus replied. He sounded weary. "I just want to see Claire."

Ooh, I was so furious! I wanted to punch them; to kick Damon sharply where it would hurt most; to scream until Kajus burst through the door. But I couldn't even glare at them. My face was frozen in what must be a relaxed expression, and when I opened my mouth, out came, "I'm fine, Kajus. Just give me a minute and I'll be out."

I'd sounded normal. Cheerful, even, and that was not alright. How could this be happening? The sort of spells that would control others' behaviour – now those were dark, and illegal as far as I knew. I doubted there were different rules here in Veestlun.

"Are you sure?" He sounded unconvinced.

No no no! "Of course," my mouth said for me. Then my hand was reaching for the door and unlatching it – when had they latched it? – and I opened the door and there he was, big and beastly and so very welcome. I wanted to burst into tears and throw myself at him, but instead I just smiled. "Were you looking for me? I came to get some linen, because Cass was taking too long." *Cass and Damon! Cass and Damon!* my mind screamed. Then I managed to shape the words, "Cass and Damon are courting, Kajus. You were right. It's a shame they're too scared of Daphne to tell the truth, huh?"

Ah, so that much I *could* say, because it didn't breach what Damon had ordered. I added a little maliciously, "They thought it was a secret, but Daphne must be the only one who doesn't know."

The door swung open wide enough to show the whole room including the two lovers. They stared sheepishly at Kajus, whose brows lowered. "Oh. I already figured that much, and I don't care. There aren't many secrets in this town. But what are you two doing in here with Claire?"

"I came to get linen," Cass said, just as Damon said, "I came to see Cass."

I saw the moment when all suspicion left Kajus. His tense posture visibly relaxed, and he set one hand against my temple. "There's blood here, Claire. You must have hit your head hard."

"Clumsy girl," Cass said with an airy laugh. "For someone with such little feet, she managed to trip over them easily enough."

Cow. "Actually I saw a rat," I blurted out.

I could feel the others' eyes on me.

"A rat?" Kajus said in dismay. "Vermin usually avoid Veestlun like the plague. Where did you see it?"

"Oh, somewhere in here," I replied just as airily as Cass had spoken. I tried to point at the two of them, but somehow my hand just moved in a dismissive wave, gesturing at the room as a whole. "Two, in fact. You wouldn't think there'd be rats in a place like this. You'd smell them." *Get it, Kajus? Damon and Cass are rats! Metaphorically speaking!*

But he mustn't have understood the familiar Enorian saying, because he just frowned. "I'll have someone come take a look later. Come on, Claire. We'll get that head bandaged. You must have hit it hard."

"It hurts," I said plaintively, which was true enough. It

did hurt, and Cass must have pulled out a good wad of hair. I'd find some way to repay that favour. Telling the whole truth would be a good start.

I followed him out of the door and down the hall, and I could hear Damon and Cass walking behind us. They were quiet, and I knew they must be scrutinizing me for signs that the influencing spell hadn't worked. I didn't know exactly what they'd done, but it was more powerful than I could have imagined.

Tell him, I screamed at myself. *Show him there's something wrong!*

But I couldn't. I couldn't do anything except...be normal.

Then Kajus stopped. "Aren't you two going to get the tablecloths?" he asked, looking over past me to where the others stood.

"Uh...of course," Cass said, tossing her long fair hair over one shoulder. "We'll just go get them. Claire, do you want to come?"

She already had one hand on my arm when I managed to pull away, because voluntarily spending time with her was *not* normal. "No thanks, Cass. You can manage it yourself, and I'm sure you and Damon want some...peace and quiet." I looked up at Kajus, almost bursting with relief. *Act normal,* Damon had said, and that actually left a lot of scope. I just needed to work out how to both act normal, and break this curse. "Kajus and I need to...talk."

"I'll come too," Damon said casually. "It doesn't take two people to get linen."

Kajus gave them both a disbelieving look. "You two are acting really strange. You're courting, I get it, and I don't care. I'm going with Claire now." And then he took me by the arm and marched me down the hall.

My hero.

9
The Lie

As I had my head gently tended to, and as the tablecloths *finally* made their way onto the many trestle tables in the Great Hall, I had plenty of opportunities to tell what I'd seen and heard. But even though everything inside me was bursting to do so, I couldn't. I couldn't raise my voice, or speak a word relating to the spells put on both me and Kajus. I couldn't even write it down…and believe me, I tried.

As instructed by Damon, I couldn't show in word or deed that anything was wrong. And when Kajus asked me what I'd wanted to speak about, all I could say was, "Oh, nothing much. I just wanted an excuse to get away from those two."

But I could do one thing, and that was stick like glue to Kajus and my family. Lunch today was casual, the sort where platters and platters of food were lined up on one main table, then everyone would pass by and take what they wanted. Just like a normal meal here in the castle, and rather like our own Enorian feasts, when we had them. I picked a purple bowl, as normal, then when I tried to head towards Kajus's table, my feet let me. Hooray!

He was sitting with Cass on his left, wearing that so-strange but appealing human form. I'd almost become used to it by now. At first it had seemed startlingly handsome, but now I could see that was just the contrast to his other,

pig-wolf face. Perhaps objectively he wasn't as handsome as
Alec or even Damon, but I still thought he suited that face
very well. But if Cassiana and Damon had their way, then he
wouldn't be wearing that face for much longer. I had to find
a way to free us both.

I sat down on his other side, smiling at him as I did so,
but with my mind buzzing frantically. "No reports today?"

"I've been told it's impolite to read at the table, especially
when there are visitors." Kajus said it lightly, but I could hear
the disgruntlement in his tone.

"Who said that?" I asked.

"My father. Daphne. Cass. Damon. About half the tanists.
The cook."

"Oh, that's a shame." Funnily enough, I had to agree
with them. Eating should be a social time. Feasts even more
so. "I'd wanted an update on the cold war between West
Arland and Sudante."

On his other side Cass made an unimpressed sound.
Kajus ignored her. "Still cold. Still a war. What more is there
to say?"

"I don't know," I said casually, but my mind was going
a mile a minute. I couldn't talk about the spell, and I had
to act normal – for me – but it seemed I could lie. What if,
as Kajus had once said, I lied in such a way that you could
read the truth from those lies? "I heard that East Arland had
something to do with it. Everyone thinks they're neutral, but
it turns out they've been orchestrating the unrest the whole
time."

His jaw dropped, revealing neat white teeth, not a
sharpened canine among them. "No! How did you find that
out? Did your father tell you?"

"Mm. Something like that. But it was to do with
boundaries between nations and their inheritances, and
who's in power. But then you go back a generation, and East
and West Arland's rulers are related. You must know that."

"It makes sense."

I studied my bowl so carefully, stirring the thick stew

with my wooden spoon, but oh so aware of Cass just feet away. Would she work out what I was saying? Kajus didn't seem to have noticed, because in my peripheral vision I could see his expression, blue eyes lit with interest.

Then suddenly his face warped and ran with black fur, and I heard the scrape of a chair pushed harshly away from the table.

"I'm finished," Cass trilled. "As scintillating as the conversation is, I think I'll go watch the finals of the archery competition."

"That doesn't start for an hour," Kajus pointed out. He didn't seem bothered by her abrupt departure, and the change that had come over him as a result."Then I'd best go get ready, hmm?"

She left, and after a few moments of silence, the two of us began snickering. "She really hates politics, doesn't she?" I commented.

"She does." He studied me, but his brows were low and his eyes narrowed. "Was any of that even true? Or did you make it up so she'd go away?"

"Mm. Both."

"So...it's true? Or it's not?"

How to work with this? I leaned in, and the urgency I wanted to inject in my tone just came out in a neutral kind of friendliness. "Oh, it's a complete lie. But West Arland and Sudante shouldn't be at war. West Arland should see that East Arland isn't their ally, and that they're the one causing all the trouble. If they do that, then maybe there can be peace." I paused. "But not between the Arlands, I suppose."

There was a silence. "Ohhkaaay..." Kajus said finally. "Are you going somewhere with this?"

Yes! I tried so hard to say that word, but all that came out was, "Politics can be messy."

"Really."

"But important," I added. "So, so important to our everyday lives."

There was another long silence, and he watched me with

a concerned expression. "Are you alright, Claire? How hard did you hit your head?"

"Oh, I didn't hit it at all." Yes! I could say that much!

Kajus threw his hands in the air. "What do you mean, you didn't hit your head? You told me that you did, and so did Cass and Damon. Claire...is something wrong?"

Yes! "Not at all," I said serenely. "Everything is completely normal with me, and especially with those two. They definitely do not have any secrets that would impact on all of us here in Veestlun, and in Rose Valley, or on you. Not at all."

"Alright..."

"But East Arland is the thing," I said cheerfully. "Apparently an ally to West Arland in their fight against Sudante, but actually trying to make things worse between them, to increase East Arland's own power because it feels unimportant and wants to, um, establish a *trading* treaty with a different kingdom. Wow, what a terrible situation there, in that area of the world, that has nothing to do with here and now."

Kajus didn't speak for a long time. Instead he sat stiffly at the table, his furred hands fisted on either side of his bowl, and his expression grim. Then finally he said in a low voice, "I don't understand what's going on, because *Cass* told me someone was up to something, but I think I'm starting to get it. Claire, are you saying that she and Damon are doing something to cause trouble between your people and ours? Something to do with their courtship, but something you can't talk about?"

"Of course they're not. No, not even slightly. Everything is perfectly normal."

"I see. And are you in danger?"

I reached up a hand to gingerly touch the raw spot where Cass had yanked out a hank of my hair. "My head hurts a little, and I'm afraid of tripping again."

Kajus let out a long, heavy breath through his nostrils. "Right. Now because everything is *normal*, you should stay with your family, or with me until everything is less... normal. Is that OK with you?"

I nodded, then finally scooped up a spoonful of stew. "Sounds good, Kajus."

"Will you come with me to talk to my father?"

"There's no need for that. I've got nothing to say." From the corner of my eye I saw a tall, pale figure approaching, and I focused on my stew. "So next time bring the reports, no matter whether you're being rude," I said lightly, and clearly enough that Damon would hear me. "Even if we're not going to marry, I do enjoy our conversations."

Damon stopped just behind me. "Are you coming to watch the archery competition?" he asked casually.

Kajus didn't give a hint of what had just been discussed. "To see how you do with the bow I restrung? Sure, why not. Are you coming, Claire?"

"Of course." I wasn't going to leave his side. Besides, Kanut would be at the competition too. Even if I couldn't explain what the problem was, maybe I could...*not* explain it, just like I had to Kajus.

I followed them to the large green field where the competition was being held. It was busy, with about twenty people lined up at one end, and a row of targets set up at the other. Spectators surrounded the field, barring the target-end. *Twang. Twang. Twang.* Arrows went flying to hit the targets in various locations, but with most clustering around the centre. But I'd expect that, as it was the archery finals, after all.

I watched without much interest as the numbers were whittled down to five, then two. Then the last few shots were fired, and the winner was called out.

It was Damon, and he took the offered trophy with a slight smile, holding it up for the crowd. But then his eyes fell on where I stood with Kajus, and that smile faltered a little. I waved cheerily, but inside I was wishing so desperately that I could just tell the whole truth.

Honestly I didn't care what went on between Damon

and Cass, except that it meant Cass stayed away from Kajus, which was worth something. But to intentionally keep him this way, just because they didn't have the courage to say what they wanted? Cowardly. And worse still, to ruin our own chances of marrying, and therefore fracture our fragile treaty...ooh, it made me *furious.*

"I wish I could shoot," I found myself saying. "Do you think anyone would mind that I'm terrible?"

"The competition's over, and the field is clear," Kajus replied, but his attention seemed elsewhere. "Why don't you have a few shots, just for fun, and I'll speak with my father just over here."

He moved away, but was still well within sight, as was Damon. I was torn between wanting to follow and knowing that I was still trapped with acting 'normal', and finally I found myself wandering over to where a couple of long bows lay on the grass, abandoned after the competition. I picked up the smallest one, testing its weight, then decided it was too heavy for me. But what did it matter anyway? I'd be lucky to hit the target.

Picking up a couple of loose arrows, I took aim then fired. *Ugh.* I hadn't even got near the target! I tried again, but had the same result. I simply didn't have the strength to send the arrow where I wanted it to go, and it made me furious. Overreaction, much?

You're upset about the spell, I reminded myself reasonably. *Not the arrow.* But it was still with irritation lending a snap to my movements that I picked up the next arrow from my waistband, then set it in position in the bow. *Pull...close one eye...oops, wrong eye. Close* other *eye...release.*

The arrow dragged past my fingers in an awkward, wobbling movement, and I realised in dismay that I'd fired Kajus's gift; the harmony oak arrow. But not to worry. My typically awful shot sent the arrow tumbling right from the bow to fall to the ground not ten feet away, half hidden in the nearby trees. "Harmony oak indeed," I said sarcastically. I stalked over to retrieve it, bent down to pick it up, then stood abruptly, swinging my fist in a downward, angry motion. Angry at the arrow, angry at the spell, angry at life right now.

Crunch. "Argh!"

The arrow's head had hit something hard behind me, just as I stood fully upright and smacked the top of my head onto something else, also hard. "Ow! Oh, I'm so sorry…"

I turned, intending to apologise to whichever poor soul had managed to get both stabbed and head-butted by me in one go, and was met by Damon's horrified face. He stood frozen right behind me, as if he'd been sneaking up to talk to me but had moved too slowly. His hand was clutched over his hip over a rapidly widening patch of dark liquid, and his lips looked white with pain, or something else. They moved in an indecipherable sound.

"Oops," I said, unable to summon up too much sympathy. "Better get that wound seen to, traitor. You wouldn't want it to fester, although you can lose a leg for all I care."

His pale face paled further, and my eyes widened as I realised what I'd said. I realised in that moment that I felt different. Looser, freer. "Traitor," I said again, my tone almost surprised. "Liar. Traitor!"

I was free! Free! What *had* I hit? Some kind of spell-pendant in his pocket? Because now I could see the liquid wasn't blood at all. It was something else, and it smelled bad, like spices mixed with offal.

I opened my mouth to scream the loudest scream known to man – and trust me, I intended to meet that goal – but I was a moment too slow. Damon lurched forward, slapping one hand over my mouth and grabbing me roughly around my upper arm with the other, then dragged me further into the stand of trees. "Shut up!" he hissed. "I mean it!"

I bit his hand, and he released me with a violent oath before grabbing me again and shaking me hard enough that my brain seemed to rattle in my skull. But I felt hot with adrenaline and fear and fury. I was so sick of being shoved around, of being used and manipulated because I wasn't strong enough in person or in personality, and that fury lent me a strength that nature never would have. I grabbed at his shirt front with one hand, and I curled the other into a fist and punched him in the gut as hard as I could, screaming like I was on fire as I did so.

Damon let out a sound like a squeaking hinge and crumpled forward – I was short, and my blow had landed a little lower than the gut. "Traitor!" I shouted again, then stomped on his foot. "Liar! Beast!"

"You little witch," he huffed out, and grabbed at me again. I wasn't sure what he intended to do at this point, but I never found out because suddenly a large figure came barrelling through, knocking Damon away from me and hard to the ground.

It was Kajus, and his face was twisted with fury that was made even fiercer by his half-shifted form as he struck Damon hard in the face once, then again, forcing his shoulders back against the damp grass. "You keep your hands off her!" he roared.

"I wasn't touching her," Damon insisted, which got about as much respect as it deserved. Kajus shook him, much in the same way as Damon had shaken me, and then somehow Damon had managed to throw his cousin off, and the two rolled over towards a nearby stream, grappling at each others' necks.

I was still shaking and panting with adrenaline, my head spinning from the chaos and from that shaking, and I couldn't think. Should I try kicking Damon again? I sure wouldn't mind, but I didn't want to get Kajus by mistake. I felt a warm hand on my shoulder and looked up to see Alec, with others behind him, both Veest and Enorian. "What happened here?" he asked me grimly. His mouth was set in a thin, white-edged line.

"Damon attacked me-" I started to say, intending to explain about the spell, the remnants of which were surely in his pocket.

But Alec didn't give me a chance to explain. He let out a howl of outrage and launched himself at the two, knocking over Damon, who'd just managed to get the upper hand.

By now we'd got quite an audience, and I heard someone say in a Veest accent, "That Enorian is attacking our Damon! Somebody help him!"

"Hold on, he was hurting our Claire," I heard Missus Streeth retort stridently. "He deserves whatever he gets!"

"Listen to me-" I began, but then a high-pitched scream sounded over the chaos, and a white and gold figure streaked past me and right towards the fighting men. It took only a moment to recognise Cassiana, and that same moment for her to raise what looked like a serving platter, then bring it crashing down on Alec's back.

"Go Cass!" I heard someone shout.

"No, she's using dark magic," I shouted, but my voice was lost over the din. And now Cass was on Alec's back, grabbing him by the hair and trying to pull him off a bloodied Damon, and Kajus was off to the side looking bemused as if he wasn't sure if he should join in.

"Help me, Kajus!" Cass shouted at him, and I saw his eyes widen. He actually moved forward as if he *would* help, and I realised in horror that while my brief enchantment might be broken, his certainly wasn't. I could see that same golden pendant swinging from her neck.

By now the tussle had moved almost to the edge of the shallow stream that ran across this part of the area, and as if in slow motion I saw Cass reach out for a fist-sized rock from the streambed.

I didn't think; I just charged. I hit her with enough force to jar my head all over again, sending her flying off Alec and into the water, with me right on top of her. My forehead whacked into her pointy chin – ouch! – but I managed to shake off the pain, urgently targeting that evil, wicked, vital little golden pendant and grabbing it in one fist.

Yank. Cass let out a squeak as the pendant came off in one go, but she was fighting me for it. I couldn't let her win. I threw the thing behind me as far as I could, looking over my shoulder as I did so, then saw that it had landed right over

Kajus's snout. Everything seemed to be happening in slow motion as he reached up to see what it was, his expression creased in lines of confusion.

Cass finally threw me off into the water and stumbled to her hands and knees, her pretty white dress sodden from the stream. She reached out one hand to Kajus, her expression beseeching. "Give me my necklace, please!"

I'd found myself sitting in the shallow water, which had quickly soaked through to my unmentionables, and I watched in horror as his hand lowered, almost as if he'd give it to her.

"No!" I shouted. "She's using dark magic, and that's an influencing spell! You need to break it!"

Around me everyone seemed to freeze, even Alec and Damon, who were still mid-wrestle.

"What did you just say?" someone demanded from behind me. I turned to see Daphne, who stood next to Kanut, my father and the Streeths. Her face was white, and her mouth tight.

"She's lying!" Cass insisted, her words garbled by tears. "Mother, don't let them damage my necklace!"

I swallowed at being the centre of attention, but rose to my feet. I *had* to make them see. "You've got to open it and break what's inside," I told Kajus urgently. "She and Damon were using one on me to stop me talking, but I broke it just five minutes ago with the arrow you gave me."

"That's a lie!" Damon insisted from his position on the ground. His face was muddied and blood-streaked, and his voice was a little slurred. "The Enorian is just jealous because the marriage was broken off, and she wants revenge. Look what she did to *me*."

"That's quite an accusation, Claire," Kanut said gravely from behind me. "Why would they do that?"

I looked around at the twenty or so people making up our audience, each wide-eyed or horrified or angry-looking, and took a deep breath to tell the whole story.

But then Kajus stretched out his hand. "I believe Claire,"

he said, and dropped the pendant on the ground, then lifted his boot. *Crunch.*

Cass let out a wail, and Damon's head slumped to hit the grass. But I was fixed on those three words, and I strode towards him, still black-furred and beastly, with my heart singing from relief. "You believed me?"

"Of course I did," he replied in surprise. "I don't know what this is all about, but I would always believe you."

"You believed *me*," I said again. And because I was jittering with the aftermath of that fight, and the fear that had come with it, and because I knew I only had so much time, I reacted. I grabbed his jacket lapels and stood up on my tiptoes to kiss him on the cheek. But he turned, and I ended up kissing him right in the middle of that hideous, piggy face. And you know what? I didn't even care.

For a moment he seemed stunned, but then just like I'd seen so many times before, the fur melted away and the form changed and suddenly I was nose to nose with the real Kajus, the one I'd wanted to marry. He blinked those blue, blue eyes and said, "Did you really just kiss my snout?"

"Um…yes," I said. "But it's not a snout anymore."

He looked down at his hands, so pale without that dark fur, then slowly reached up to his bare human face, feeling the skin and changed shape under his hand. Those blue eyes blinked, and he let out a deep, slow breath as he looked across to where his cousin lay, battered and bruised, and to where Cass sat weeping in the stream. "I think you'd better tell us what's going on."

"I think you'd better," Kanut agreed ominously. But he wasn't speaking to me; he was speaking to the other two.

Somebody was in trouble, but this time it wasn't me.

10
Cutie and the Veest

Late that night Kajus and I sat quietly on one of the stone balconies that led from the back of the castle into the orchard where he'd first tried to teach me to shoot. The scent of roses filled the air just as it had since I'd arrived. But then it was summer, and the flowers were in bloom. His hand – his bare, warm, hairless hand – was loosely held in mine, and he seemed to carry the same weariness that I felt. Weariness, but something more too.

"I know it's true," he said finally, "and that Cass and Damon deserve to be imprisoned for what they did. But it's so hard to accept that my own cousin would do such a thing to me, and for so long."

"I know," I said.

"And from such a young age? Claire, they were practically children when they bought those influencing spells. They shouldn't have been able to get them! But they knew they were illegal."

"Yes, they did."

"And then to try to put the spell on my own father, so that he'd make Damon a tanist? And then to use my hair by mistake?" Kajus shook his head in disgust. "And then they realised that I was stuck in this horrible half-shifted form, and they didn't try to free me. Not once."

I would have spoken, but he continued more fervently, "I remember the day I couldn't change back. I remember Cass coming up to me and saying something like, 'You think I'm lovely, don't you Kajus?' And of course I agreed, but I remember in that moment feeling like I'd had a revelation, like I *did* think she was lovely but maybe hadn't noticed before. That must have been the day she'd started wearing the spell.

"And then she'd come up to me now and then even in my beastly form, and she'd say things like, 'I want you to think of me all the time' or 'You want to please me, don't you? I'm special to you.' And she'd been resetting the spell, trying to ensure it didn't wear off, so I didn't change forms before the time was up!"

"What a witch," I said fervently. Because really, she was. And Damon was worse, because he'd been family, and he should have been better. He'd even shared a room with Kajus for years and years, and had kept silent on any night-time changes. He and Cass together had created this curse – this cage – and they'd done it out of selfishness.

"I know, right?" Kajus waved his free hand expressively through the air. "And then to attack you like they did? They deserve to be imprisoned. They're worse than traitors, and fear is not an excuse for what they did!"

"Mm," I agreed thoughtfully. "And neither is love." I thought back to earlier, to when the truth had all finally come out, and to when Cass had tearfully spilled her whole story – or her version of the truth, anyway. Damon had mostly just sat there in stoic silence. I remembered how she'd said, *We love each other*, and *we did it for love*.

"What?"

"They said they did all this for love, but they can't have loved each other that much if they let their fear stop them from being honest. What was the worst that could have happened?"

Kajus seemed to ponder this. "Daphne could have forced Cassiana into a betrothal with someone else. Damon too, maybe."

"Oh. Enorians don't tend to do forced betrothals." I scowled. "Then they should've just eloped. Surely they would have been allowed back eventually?"

He looked down at my hand in his, my skin so much darker than his own, then smiled up at me. "Probably. But one good thing did come out of it. If they hadn't put the spell on me, which had the side-effect of stopping me changing forms, then I never would have met you, because Father wouldn't have set up things as he did. Then you never would have broken the spell."

I felt my cheeks heat, because I knew what he was referring to. "You know the kiss didn't break the spell," I said, not for the first time. "It was just a coincidence, because even though it was broken already with the pendant, and even though you'd had the help from that Wyse remedy, you still had to make the choice to change forms."

"I choose to believe you broke it," Kajus countered with a smile, "and so that's how it is."

"If you say so."

"I do."

And then he leaned down and looked at me for a long moment, then at my lips so close to his. Then he leaned in further and-

"*Ahem!*"

We both jolted upright, then turned to see both our fathers standing not five feet away. I hadn't even heard them approach. Kanut looked as though he was trying to appear stern, but a smile was creeping in at the edges of his mouth. My father looked thoughtful.

"Good news," my father said mildly. "With today's revelations, the opposition to the treaty has stepped down. We can stay in Rose Valley as planned, with or without any marriage. We just have to give a share of any crops as rent, starting next year."

"Oh," Kajus and I said in unison. I felt my cheeks heat, then turned to see him looking at me.

"What if we still want to marry?" he asked.

Now Kanut did let out a short laugh. "Then that's a different story, boy, and no one's surprised. But we'll talk later. Come on in, it's dinner time."

And the rest, as they say, is history. Damon and Cassiana were never tried for their crimes. Instead they 'somehow' escaped in the night, presumably having run off to make a life together. Kajus thought Daphne had let them out, and didn't care. I figured they should have just done that in the first place and saved everyone a lot of trouble – but then as my betrothed says, if they had done things right, maybe we never would have met, and that would have been a tragedy.

Yes, you can say it. Awww.

As I write this, there's another tragedy that's recently been averted. Tabitha helped Alec tend his wounds, and decided that he was a lot kinder and better-looking than beastly Ned. Alec decided that yes, Tabitha was extremely pretty in spite of the slight age difference, and that he wouldn't mind taking her away from said beast. Good for them both, and definitely good for me. One occasionally-hairy monster in the family is enough.

The Enorians settled comfortably in Rose Valley, and I went with them at first. But over the last few months I've moved back and forth between Veestlun and the valley along with Father, who's become the official Veest emissary, and who's also courting Missus Babic. I still find her formidable, but Father doesn't, and that's all that matters.

Things are going well enough that there'll be another combined Veest-Enorian festival this year. Except this time, we Enorians are hosting.

Gulp. *There's sure to be drama, chaos, and more than a little cake. All in all, not a bad ending. But as for Kajus and I, our life is just beginning. Because this year...we get married for real.*

The end of Claire's story, but not the end of Fairytale Memoirs. Turn the page for an excerpt from The Mostly Forgotten Memoirs of Rose-Red - another non-traditional, fun take on a classic tale.

Dear Reader,

I'm not sure where the idea for *Gifted* came from. Probably from one of the many, many, many fairytale iterations out there; mixed with a werewolf movie or two. But something about the idea stuck with me, and after several revisions of what I was calling 'Cutie and the Veest', I finally had something I wasn't ashamed for people to read. (Aim high, I say.)

Gifted is character-based rather than action-based, at least until the end, and I enjoyed playing with this new topic of arranged marriages, fairytale-style. Arranged marriages for money, land or peace are something humans have done for a long time, and while it's completely different from the usual modern, Western experience, it was a reality that girls Claire's age or even younger would have faced. Fortunately I can give my own characters a happily-ever-after, but real life is seldom so straightforward.

That's why fiction can be such great fun. For more stories like this one, check out my website **mmarinanbooks.com.**

Also, if you enjoyed this story, please leave a review at your favourite website. They really make a difference to authors being able to continue producing. (If you didn't like the story, feel free to forget you ever read it. Thank you.)

The Mostly Forgotten Memoirs of Rose Red

A Fairytale Memoirs Novel

M. MARINAN

The Mostly Forgotten Memoirs of Rose Red

EXCERPT

Just outside the village of Leewhey, Danvia,
1673 FTE (fairytale era)

Thump.

"Ignore it," Mother called from across the cottage where she sat peeling carrots in front of the fire. It was late autumn, but felt more like winter so the fire was a necessity. "It'll just be a gnome again, and I don't want the cold getting inside."

"Never mind the cold," I muttered. I was sitting on a stool near the small table we used for everything, a large blanket draped over me, the stool *and* the table. In theory I was mending it, but in reality I was enjoying keeping my legs warm. We still needed to buy new winter gowns and stockings, but the money had yet to materialize. "I don't want the *gnome* getting inside. It was hard enough getting it out the first time."

My twin sister Snow, who was sitting opposite me at the table – *actually* mending her part of the blanket – giggled, and Mother lifted her head sharply. "What was that, Rosaline?"

"She was just agreeing that the door should stay shut," Snow called across to her, and I smiled at her in relief. As much as we both loved her, we knew Mother's sense of humour had been very poor since Father died two summers earlier, but then perhaps losing everything would do that to you. And the way she'd called me by my full name rather than my commonly used nickname? Not a good sign.

"Of course it should," Mother agreed, frowning. Her fine blonde brows knit above her nose, and she squinted irritably at the pile of orange shavings in front of her. "I don't believe this knife is working very well. I'd vow I have more peel than carrot left over, and these carrots were not cheap!"

But then she'd insisted on buying the more expensive orange carrots that we always had when Father was alive, when the standard purple carrots were a fraction of the price. I opened my mouth to say as much, but Snow gave me a warning glance. "I'll sharpen it for you, Mother," she called back, climbing out from under the blanket to fetch the whetstone from the kitchen area. And by area, I meant corner of the room that served for everything except our beds.

"I'll do it," I said, regretting my previous snarkiness. "I'm better with the whetstone."

"All the more reason for me to practice," Snow retorted practically.

Fair point. I focussed back on the blanket – after all, we wouldn't be paid for mending until we actually *did* the mending – until another loud noise interfered with my concentration.

BANG BANG THUMP.

This time someone was definitely outside the door. "That's not a gnome," I called. "Snow, will you get it?"

But she'd already gone to the door. I felt the wash of cold air as it opened, heard Snow gasp, and then a moment later heard the *clunk* of the door slamming shut.

"Who was it?" Mother asked impatiently. "Not another peddler, surely? They must see we're in no position to buy trinkets."

"Um…" Snow had turned as pale as her blonde hair, and stood wide-eyed, her back pressed up flat against the door as if to hold it shut. "It's not a peddler."

"I'm sorry," a muffled, deep voice called through the thin wood of the door. "I didn't mean to frighten you. It's just this snow…"

Suddenly on alert, Mother and I exchanged wary glances. Three females out in the woods, not even within shouting distance of the village, and none of us very tall or strong or trained in the warrior arts…

"It's a *man*," Mother said tightly. "No one you know, Snow?"

She shook her head, then muttered something.

"What?" Mother asked.

But I'd been closer, and I'd heard what she'd said. Sort of. "Did you just say it's a *bear*?"

"Please?" the person outside begged. He did have a *very* deep voice. "I can't feel my feet. I swear I'll pay you back, I just need to defrost!"

"Don't be silly," Mother scolded me. "Bears can't talk. Who is it, Snow?" She put down the carrots but kept the knife, shaking out her full skirts as she rose to her feet. We might be as poor as church mice now, but my mother still carried herself like a lady. (Or a former merchant's wife who *wanted* to be a lady. Same thing.)

I followed her to the door, and Snow finally stepped away. "But it *is* a bear," she whispered. "A brown bear, as big as the doorway. And it *was* talking."

"I *am* talking!" the possibly-a-bear called through the door. "And I can't help being a bear. I'm not normally like this, I swear! I'm-" And here the unknown person dissolved into a coughing fit.

"By the king's crown," I whispered back, my voice lower. Clearly our visitor had good hearing. "It has to be someone under a curse! And you know that if we turn away someone in need then *we'll* have the curse turn back on us-"

"That only happens if it's a Wyse woman testing you," Mother said practically. "Like with that prince in Sudante a few years back. *This* could be another disaster waiting to happen. You both heard about that possessed wolf attacking Grandmother Hood last spring."

"I'm not going to eat you!" the bear-person cried from outside the door. "I'm not a cannibal! I'm-" And he broke into yet another coughing fit. It appeared that our visitor was unable to say exactly what the problem was, and I didn't know whether that made me more scared or excited.

I moved to grab our most solid frying pan, the one made of cast iron with a smoke-blackened base. "What should we do?" I whispered.

Snow's face was still white, but her grey-green eyes were intent. "We should let him in. I'm sure of it."

There was something to her tone that made Mother and I pay attention. See, besides being as sweet-natured as she was pretty (and Snow was *very* pretty) my sister also had...well, we called it a gift from God, others called it the second sight, and the very superstitious called it witchcraft. Sometimes she just *knew* things. Always had, right from a young age, and we'd learned to trust her when she got that look on her face.

Mother and I looked at each other, and Mother finally sighed, running a hand over her face as if tired. "Very well, but let him be warned," and here she raised her voice, "that any shenanigans and his fur will be warming our hearth."

Snow gave her a reproachful look, then opened the door. Surprise surprise, there *was* a bear standing there on his hind legs. It – he – was big and brown with shaggy fur dusted with snow from our unseasonably cold autumn. He blinked his small brown eyes a few times as if startled by the sight before him, then bent over into what turned out to be a sort of bow. "Thank you...good ladies," the bear said fervently. "You have no idea how much I appreciate this."

I saw Mother brighten at being called a lady. Even when

Father was alive, she hadn't had the title to be named such; just the money. She stepped back, allowing the creature in. A moment later I did the same, and the bear shuffled forward, paused to turn sideways so it could fit through the door, then slumped onto the mat-covered earth of the cottage floor. I closed the door behind him and we waited for him to get up, or to say something further (because really, a talking bear *is* rather exciting), but his eyes rolled back in his head and he fell over sideways. *Thump.*

There was a moment of silence where I noted the matted, bloodied fur underneath that dusting of melting snow, and it occurred to me that perhaps the bear wouldn't make it, under a curse or no. If so, Mother would have her hearth warmer after all. "Bags not skinning him," I said dryly.

It was time for bed, and Mother was still scolding me for carelessly speaking about a guest, or more importantly a *conscious* guest. Snow had given me a reproachful look that pricked my conscience, but it was the bear-man's expression of horror that really had me embarrassed. "I didn't mean it," I'd told him honestly. "We wouldn't have done that, if you'd died. We would have buried you." After winter, when the ground was softer.

I don't know if he believed me, but he said that he did. Snow had spotted his wound – a rather nasty arrow one at that – and was cooing over him like he was a sweet little lamb or a unicorn rather than a giant carnivore. He'd lapped it up, and was even now snuggled under the blanket we'd been mending for Mistress Swanpoel's gardener, watching her with a slightly awed expression. But then as I said before, Snow was very pretty. She wasn't particularly short, but her delicacy made it seem like she was, and even with her fair colouring she never flushed unattractively pink. I was her twin – *not* identical, you understand – and I was darker and…well, heartier, with a tendency to flush deep red with embarrassment, anger, over-exercise…hence the nickname.

Mother finally stopped scolding me, turning to follow my

131

gaze where it was fixed on Snow and the bear. She frowned a little, then shrugged. "It can't do any harm for him to take a fancy to her. And who knows? Perhaps he's rich."

My eyebrows shot up, and she scowled at me. "Oh, don't look at me like that, Rose-Red. A potential suitor is a potential suitor. I meant *after* the curse is broken."

Famous words from my mother, who was convinced that a good marriage guaranteed lifelong happiness. Then perhaps it had for her, or at least until Father died and we found out he hadn't been as good with money as we'd assumed. "Or he could just as easily be a pauper," I pointed out.

Mother lifted her chin. "Then we've made a fine friend to help us through this second winter, have we not?"

I couldn't argue with that. Last winter had been... not fun.

We spent the night tending the bear's wounds. Or rather, I spent an hour binding the wounds with Snow looking on and making sympathetic noises. Mother had long since gone to bed. Then I went to bed, and Snow stayed with the bear 'making sure he was alright'.

Good for her, but I'd rather have a decent night's sleep.

In the morning the bear was still slumped in a furry pile in front of the fire. Now before you think that was actually a convenient (and warm) chair for us, I should say that our cottage had only two rooms. After Father died – well, his debts were sizeable, and we had to go from being comfortably well-off commoners to being poor ones. It's a cliché, poor widow lives in tiny cottage in the woods with her young daughters, but the truth is that it happens so often. Especially as there are so few things that a woman can respectably do to earn money. Without our dowries, Snow and I, having just turned eighteen, were more appealing to people as a hired 'escort' than for marriage now. And by 'escort' I mean...well, if you don't know, then I certainly won't be explaining it to you. But we actually had a few of those dishonourable offers when

Father first died and we had to come here where the living was cheaper. I tell you, if I had the funds, I would start up a business that employed widows or girls without dowries for good work!

Sorry, got distracted. Yes, the world is unfair, but it doesn't do anyone any good to dwell on its unchangeable evils. Anyway, the whole point of what I just said was that the darned bear took up a lot of room. Not exactly convenient, but we couldn't kick some poor person out into the snow just because they weren't currently human.

When the bear finally woke up we gave him a bowl of water and some leftover stew. He mumbled his thanks, and Snow and I watched in amazement as he carefully picked up the wooden bowl and ate it with as much manners as the average street urchin, which is rather more than your average bear has. "Thank you," he said when he'd finished, setting the bowl down on the floor and then slumping as though exhausted. "I feel as though I haven't eaten in an age."

"Were you hibernating?" Snow asked him.

The bear looked at her blankly, and I cut in. "If he was hibernating, then he'd be a lot thinner. Bears don't eat while they hibernate."

"Actually," the bear said apologetically, "I wouldn't have gone into hibernation quite yet, as it's technically still autumn...or supposed to be, anyway. Except I'm not really a-" And he collapsed into another coughing fit. I hadn't even realised bears could cough, yet here it was.

"Here, have some water," Snow suggested, offering up the bowl.

"Thank you kindly," the bear said again, giving her what might have been a warm look. Hard to tell with all that fur. He slurped at the water, getting a bit of it over his coat, then knocked the bowl with his plate-sized paw, spilling the whole thing over his front. "Oh my. I'm dreadfully sorry. It's these paws, you understand. I'm not used to them, because I'm not usually a-" And here he burst into another uncontrollable coughing fit.

133

"You're not usually a bear," I said clearly. "That's what you're trying to say, right?"

The bear nodded, then clapped a paw over its mouth. "I do believe I can't say it. The thing that you just said."

"What, that you're not really a bear?" Snow asked sweetly.

He went to speak again...cue another coughing fit.

"Oh dear," Snow said sincerely. "You needn't keep trying to speak, but I'd venture a guess you're cursed, are you not?"

A furry nod.

"And you're actually human."

An *emphatic* furry nod – although really, we'd worked it out by then.

"Oh, good," Mother said from behind us, having just entered the room. "Then perhaps we might introduce ourselves, as you are currently our guest? I am Madame Lena, a widow, and these are my twin daughters, Snow-White and Rose-Red." That was how everyone always said our names, Snow's first. Perhaps it just sounded better that way.

But I saw the bear's surprise at the knowledge we were not just sisters, but twins (the colour difference got them every time, or perhaps he was surprised by our rather literal names), and then he remembered his manners and touched a paw to his own chest in a gentlemanly manner. "I am- COUGH COUGH COUGH COUGH..."

To cut a long story short, we figured out that he couldn't speak directly about the curse, *or* about who he was. Using nods for yes, head shakes for no, we did work out that a) he might know how to break the curse, b) he certainly couldn't explain it to us, and c) his name was something like Edward or Edgar, but even us calling him those names set off coughing fits. And let me tell you, a persistently coughing bear is not a fun companion, even one who apologises after each fit.

"Might we give you a nickname?" Snow asked. "We can't keep calling you 'the bear' since it seems rather disrespectful."

"What, like 'Hairy'?" he suggested.

Snow giggled – showing she'd got the joke, where Mother

and I certainly hadn't – and said, "I was thinking more like 'Eddie'. That's a nice friendly name, and perhaps not too far from your own."

"If you like Eddie, then so do I," the bear agreed promptly. The newly named Eddie gave Snow a look I could only call gooey, which was strange to say the least on a face like his. Snow had made another conquest. That fragile blonde prettiness would do it every time. Still, if you're going to have a giant predator in your house, better to have one that *likes* you, right?

An hour later Eddie was still being cared for by Snow, and Mother had got back onto the mending. That left me to do my usual chores, because someone had to. "I'll go and get firewood," I told the room at large.

Snow didn't respond. Mother said, "Please get some eggs at the market while you're out," without looking up.

"But we haven't finished mending anything yet," I pointed out. "We don't have any money."

Suddenly I had everyone's attention, and I felt my cheeks heat. Of course Mother and Snow knew our financial situation, but somehow I felt embarrassed that now Eddie did too.

"I darned the rip in Master Jameson's jacket last night while I was tending Eddie," Snow said. "It's by the door. That'll be enough for half a dozen eggs."

She'd fixed it last night, while she'd been up and tending a talking bear, and while I'd probably been snoring obliviously. "Oh. Thanks."

I grabbed the jacket, a large basket, and my faded blue winter cloak, then headed out the doorThe day was as cold as expected, with the cloudy grey sky visible through the burnt-orange leaves of the forest surrounding our small property. Luckily it was neither raining nor snowing, so I pulled my warm hood down around my face, then began to stride along the well-trodden, muddy path leading towards the village of Leewhey. It would be nice to chat with a few villagers I hadn't seen since the cold set in, then I could collect firewood on my way home.

Half an hour later I'd reached the village, had offloaded the jacket to Mistress Agnes Jameson, and was happily accepting the hot soup she'd offered me in exchange for one less egg. "It's cold out," she told me, "even though your cheeks are red as ever, Miss Rose-Red. And why were you walking that path alone today, I ask?"

I didn't take offense at her nosiness. Agnes was like most of the village women in that she lived for gossip, but was kind-hearted enough for me to overlook the habit. "Snow needs to stay in the warm today," I replied, carefully skirting around the truth. I didn't want to tell anyone about Eddie, not until he explicitly said we could. "But I don't mind coming out."

Agnes clucked her tongue. "Of course Snow would feel the chill; dainty, lovely girl that she is. Well, you just watch your step out in those woods, and no talking to strangers, you hear?"

I bit back my response that Snow was tougher than she looked, and focused on the second part of her comment. "What strangers could there possibly be?" I asked, briefly forgetting a certain talking bear. "It's a village of two hundred people."

She raised her chin loftily, for a moment looking more like a duchess than a butcher's wife. "You haven't heard?"

"Haven't heard what?"

She leaned in towards me, her tone taking on a conspiratorial air. "Mistress Joan told me that one of the royal princes was seen about the area this morning. Riding a fine black horse, he was, along with half a dozen guards. Now what do you have to say about *that*?"

I blinked. "A prince? Like, a prince of Danvia?"

"Yes, a prince of Danvia!" Agnes said with some exasperation. "We're not likely to receive any foreign princes all the way out here, are we?"

"I suppose not." I considered that for a moment. Thanks to village gossip I knew that our king, Xavier, had one daughter and two sons. I'd even seen a painting of the royal family, when I'd delivered goods to a local, wealthy household. It had been a faded image of a golden-haired couple surrounded by a trio of golden-haired children. The littlest had the round cheeks of an infant. But it figured the princes were no longer children, if one was able to ride out here alone. Barring the guards, of course.

She seemed to want more of a response than that, so I added, "You don't need to worry. If I run into anyone in the forest, I won't stop to chat."

I took my time walking back home, pausing every now and then to pick up sticks for firewood and add them to my basket next to the precious eggs. The sticks were all completely sodden from the freezing rain, but if we put them at the back of the cottage they'd hopefully dry out before we actually needed to use them. Last winter we'd run out of wood before the weather began to warm in spring, and let me tell you, that hadn't been fun.

I was caught up in memories of that awful winter, and I almost didn't hear the hoofbeats until it was too late.

"Look out!" I heard a male voice shout, and I threw myself instinctively off the dirt path, landing heavily in a half-frozen fern. Then what seemed like a dozen horses thundered past on the narrow route, sending mud splattering up all over my well-worn grey dress and cloak.

"Watch where you're going!" I hollered after them, and I'd swear I heard a faint, "*Sorry!*" hollered back. But perhaps that was just wishful thinking, because I did know what I *had* seen – and that was the king's coat-of-arms on those horses.

Still, I muttered to myself as I clambered to my feet. That mud was *everywhere*, and so were the sticks from my basket… and the eggs.

On my oath, I was *not* happy.

"It could have been worse," Snow told me matter-of-factly once I'd returned home. "You might have lost all the eggs, not just two. You might have been trampled, or you might have broken a limb. At least now you've got a good story to tell next time you're in the village."

"That I almost got run over by a royal guard?" I retorted, beginning to see the humour in the situation. "I don't know where they were going in such a hurry, Snow, but at least I can say they were polite. Where's Eddie?"

"He's excused himself for a few moments."

My mind was blank until I realised what she meant. Bears couldn't use privies, surely? "Oh. Okay."

Privy-user or not, Eddie stayed another two nights, then politely thanked us for our help and left. We thought he'd gone permanently, and Snow cried because she missed him. I didn't cry, but I saw where she was coming from. He had turned out to be thoughtful, curious and clever, which is a hard combination to find in a human, let alone a woodland creature. We didn't ask him any more about his origins, though. He wouldn't have been the first person to get on the wrong side of a witch or one of the nastier Wyse people. Both of those were notoriously easy to offend, and known to overreact when they were offended.

We all got back to our usual chores, me outside, while Mother sewed for wealthier people with poor stitching ability, and Snow did the inside chores. She actually liked them, believe it or not. Mind you, she thought the same thing about the jobs I much preferred – shovelling snow, chopping wood, gutting the various animals we caught in our traps. And yes, I always checked that they weren't talking ones before I turned them into dinner.

One day when that early run of snow had melted and the weather had gone from winter-frigid to merely autumn-unpleasant, Snow and I were coming home from our weekly trip to the market in the nearby village of Leewhey. We were about halfway home, in the deepest part of the woods when we heard an odd, high-pitched whine. It sounded like a cross between the miller's dog complaining at being left alone and Mother when she was in a bad mood. We decided to check it out, and not far from the path we found him – a dwarf trapped by his over-long beard in the crevice of a tree.

Now you should know this about dwarves. They are not small humans; they are something else entirely, a slightly supernatural race famously obsessed with gold. We didn't see many of them around here. They preferred to live in groups of their own kind in places far from humans, doing whatever it was they did to pass the time.

The funny thing was, I had never seen a single female dwarf. Someone had suggested that they kept their females locked away for religious reasons, while someone else had said perhaps that there were only a few females who each had dozens of babies, like cats. I liked the idea that the females had beards too, and that was why you couldn't tell which was which.

Anyway, the few dwarves I had met had been polite but uninterested in what the huge human people might be doing. This one? He wasn't so polite.

When he saw us he shrieked, "For the love of Od, I've been stuck here for hours! What are you staring at? Get me out of here NOW!"

Snow and I exchanged startled glances. "Goodness," Snow murmured under her breath. "Someone's forgotten their manners."

The dwarf clearly had better hearing than we'd expected, because his face twisted into even more of a scowl than before. "As if you'd be any better in such a situation! Help me!"

My sister and I exchanged another glance, this one saying without words that even though his attitude was rotten, we'd still help him. We'd been raised to treat people with respect even if they didn't deserve it, and this dwarf *definitely* didn't deserve it.

We stepped forward, and Snow tried to unwind the rough brown beard from where it was snagged on the tree, but it seemed to be stuck fast. I took a closer look. "Wow, you've really got it stuck in there. How did you manage that?"

The dwarf gave me a horrible sneer, and I revised my

opinion of dwarves in general being polite and a little bit cute. This one had eyes like little black coals, and I was willing to bet even on such short acquaintance that his heart was just the same. "Stupid, milk-faced human! It doesn't matter *how* it got in there, just that it needs to get out! I have somewhere to be, and I don't have time for your chitchat!"

Honestly, he was an inch away from a kick in the shin rather than the *help* he needed, but Snow saw the look on my face and put a restraining hand on my arm. "If we don't get him out, he could freeze, or get eaten by something."

And refusing to help him would make us murderers by neglect. I sighed heavily. "Fine." So Snow and I very graciously spent a good ten minutes trying to get that beard away from the tree, the anonymous dwarf impatiently pushing us along the whole time. I even tried to pull off the branch it was stuck on, but couldn't make it budge.

"It's no good," I finally admitted. "Snow, I'll have to go home and get my saw."

"Home?" the dwarf squawked. "How far is that?"

"Half an hour each way from here," my sister replied.

"No! That won't do at all!" he shouted. "The two of you fools can't even do a simple thing between you?"

Forget a kick in the shin, this guy needed a kick in the teeth. And with his low height, it would be an easy enough target. No one had *ever* been so rude to me before, especially without provocation from me. (Which yes, once in a while I might provide). "Forget it," I said to Snow. "Let's go. He got himself in there, he can get himself out."

But there was a strange, martial light in Snow's eyes, an expression I hadn't seen before since she usually had the patience of a saint. (One of the gentler ones, not a fire and brimstone one). "Oh, no," she said gently. "I'll help him. I'll help him right now." And then she pulled out a pair of scissors from her pocket and *snip!* Cut off the end of the beard. The dwarf was free all right, but his beard was a good three inches shorter.

There was a moment where we all just stared at the beard

with its now blunt end, and then Snow slipped the scissors back in her pocket. "You're welcome."

The dwarf's face reddened and his black eyes bulged as he studied the slightly shorter beard. He looked like he was about to implode with anger, like we'd killed his pet puppy. "You dared cut my marvellous beard? Do you have any idea how long this took to grow?"

I considered the question. "Seventy years?"

The dwarf just glared. "Seventy! *Seventy*!?"

"I think perhaps the question was rhetorical," Snow murmured to me in an aside.

"Oh." But did that mean I had guessed too high, or too low? None of the human men I knew had managed a beard past their mid-chest, and personally I found that quite unappealing. They tended to get big and fluffy, and it made me want to grab a pair of hedge clippers and trim them like topiary.

"Stupid girl," the dwarf spat. "Stupid, oversized, red-faced beast."

My eyebrows shot up along with my temper, but Snow set her hand on my arm. "Just let him go."

"Yellow-haired hag," he added with a dark look at Snow. I choked back a cry of indignation mixed with laughter – a hag, really? – but managed to keep my mouth shut while he grabbed a small, heavy-looking bag that had been at his feet. There was a *chink* of coins as he picked it up, then he began stalking away, muttering to himself the whole time.

I waited for a few moments until he was almost out of sight around the path, then called, "Have a nice day!"

The dwarf didn't stop walking, but he *did* take the time to make a certain rude hand gesture in our direction. Snow let out a cry of dismay.

"Same to you, jackanapes!" I shouted furiously. "See if we ever help you again!"

But then he was gone, and my sister turned to me with what was for her a disapproving expression. "Jackanapes?"

"He called you a yellow-haired hag, and me a beast! We

might have saved his life, Snow. If he hadn't got out of that tree, he could have been eaten by something, or else frozen to death!"

"Very well, he was a jackanapes," Snow agreed. She sighed. "What a ridiculous, rude little man. I tell you, I had a mind to just leave him there!"

I stared at her. Snow, admitting to angry feelings? "Me too!"

"Never would have done it though."

I gave a sigh. "Afraid not. You just shortened his beautiful beard from five inches past his toes to a mere two inches past. Wicked girl."

She gave a mock sorrowful look. "I am indeed."

As if. Feeling quite unreasonably cheered up, I slipped my arm through hers and headed home. There was nothing like seeing someone else's self-induced misery to make you feel better about your own life.

About a week after the beard incident, a big brown shape ambled out of the woods.

"Eddie!" Snow cheered, running to wrap her arms around his big fuzzy neck. "You're back."

"Just to visit, mind," Eddie said apologetically. "I still need to focus on breaking the- *cough, cough, cough...*"

The unmentionable thing, which meant he'd had no luck breaking the curse. "Hi, Eddie."

"Hello, Rose," he replied, finally dragging his gaze away from Snow. "Are you well?"

"Well enough."

We chatted a little more, and then Snow said, "You're just in time for dinner!"

Eddie looked sheepish, which said to me that he'd smelled the dinner a mile away, but came in to eat. While he and Snow chatted by the fire, Mother and I spoke quietly.

"Some kind of noble, do you think?" I suggested, glancing across the room.

Mother followed my gaze. "He appears well-bred," she

agreed thoughtfully. "Or at least his manners imply a gentle upbringing."

Perhaps not too gentle, I pondered, as he'd not shown a hint of disdain for our admittedly simple home. But maybe if you were turned into a bear and essentially went around naked all the time and were shot at by people you once considered friends (more guessing about the wounds) then you'd realise that nothing was really beneath you anymore. Except, perhaps, for being turned into a rug.

Mother was still watching Snow and Eddie where they sat whispering on the woven rug, Snow with her hand cupped over Eddie's fuzzy ear, and Eddie with an expression of delight. "They certainly seem to get on well," she commented. "I wonder if it will last?"

Want to read more?
For a list of ebook and print retailers,
go to **mmarinanbooks.com**